OPPOSING TEAMS (RIVALS)

SCOTIA STORMS

CATHRYN FOX

Discover other titles by Cathryn Fox at www.cathrynfox.com. Please sign up for Cathryn's Newsletter for freebies, ebooks, news and contests: https://app.mailerlite.com/webforms/landing/c1f8n1
ISBN ebook : 978-1-998943-41-8
ISBN Print: 978-1-998943-45-6

KAI

I stand outside the rink chatting with Bree—a girl I met at Scotia Academy my freshman year—when Theo Wagner's grating voice cuts into my thoughts and rakes down my spine like sandpaper. Everything inside me tightens as I listen to him boast about his own accomplishments—and how he's been scouted by Boston Bucks. Sure, it's okay to be proud of achieving all his goals, but does he need to call down other players—on my team—just to make himself look better? What a fucking asshole.

I momentarily tear my gaze away from Bree and glance to my left. That's when my gaze locks with Theo's, and everything inside me wants to wipe the smirk off his face—with my fist.

"Hey, are you okay?" Bree asks, and touches my arm to bring my attention back to her.

I turn, but not before Theo aims his smirk my way. "Yeah."

"Do you know that guy?" she asks, hugging herself against the damp chill this late September night as she glances around me to see Theo standing there like the smug asshole he is, as his groupies—men and women alike—surround him and look up at him like he's going to be NHL's next greatest thing.

I snort. "Yeah, I know him." Shit, Theo and I go way back, and as much as I'd like to introduce my fist to his face as he talks shit about one of our players, I don't. My fist to his pretty-boy face is what got me a three-game suspension while I was still in high school.

Theo grew up in Greenwood. I grew up a couple miles away in Middleton. We came from rival schools. Not much has changed since we moved to Halifax. He now attends Kingston College, which is just down the street from Scotia Academy. We've been opponents for as long as I can remember, but I'm not going to get into an altercation with him now and risk a suspension. Making it to the NHL is too damn important to me. It's my sole focus, and I can't let anyone or anything get in the way. I owe it to Coop. His death can't be for nothing.

Theo laughs and I can't help but look as he pulls a cigarette from his pocket and lights it. What kind of an NHL wannabe smokes, for Christ's sake? I just shake my head at him, and the smile fades from his face.

That's when I realize my mistake. The fucker was looking for a reaction, a reason to start something between us. Damned if I didn't just give it to him. I straighten to my full height. All righty then. Here we go.

"Hey Kai, you got a problem with me?"

Bree's eyes go big. "Let's go inside," she says and takes my arm. She gives me a tug and I'm about to follow—do I really want to waste my energy on a douche bag like Theo? No, I don't. Years ago, however, I'd had no choice but to get involved. His girlfriend was mad at Theo and thought it would be fun to hit on a member of the opposing team—me —while he watched. I didn't want anything to do with the game she was playing, but that didn't stop her from throwing her arms around me in the parking lot after a game.

That's when the shit hit the fan and Theo brought up my driving skills and blatantly laughed about the accident that killed my best friend Cooper. *Buddy murderer.* That's what he fucking called me. I'm usually good at burying things and keeping my temper in check, but that day, well, he'd pushed all the right buttons. I ended up with a suspension. He ended up with two broken ribs that sidelined him for four games, and a missing tooth. That was just a bonus.

"Hey, don't let him drive you home after the game," Theo blurts out to Bree seconds before I enter the sports complex. I stop dead in my tracks. Oh no, he fucking didn't. I take a deep breath, but it does little to cool the anger surging through me.

"Kai?" Bree questions, as a bunch of her friends come running up to join us, completely oblivious to the tension sparking in the night air. Christ, any second now I expect to see a light-ning storm overhead.

"Good luck tonight, Kai," Summer says and throws her arms around me for a hug. I hug her back, even though every muscle in my body is tense. "Whoa, are you okay?" She inches back, her eyes full of worry as she follows my gaze to Theo. "What's going on?" she asks, turning her attention to Bree. Theo and I square off, and Bree whispers back that she doesn't know. Honestly, why would she know?

Bree and I have known each other for three years, having met our freshman year of college, but I don't go around telling people I was driving one stormy night, and went off the road and killed my best friend. Who goes around talking about that? I don't know, but what I do know is it should have been me who died that night. Cooper was the best guy I know—knew—and didn't deserve to die. He had so many friends, was liked by everyone and he had dreams, big dreams, like the two of us going off to the NHL together. Even though I don't think I deserve the NHL now, I'm doing it to keep Coop's dream alive.

"Yeah, I actually think you do have a problem, Ward," Theo blurts out after taking a long pull from his cigarette and filling the air with smoke. How does he care so little about his body, or his game?

"No problem," I force myself to say.

Keep the fight for the rink, Kai.

My gaze strays to the petite, pretty girl shifting nervously beside Theo. I've seen her around before, here and back home. She went to high school with Theo and now she's on the douche bag's arm before and after every game. Half the time I don't even think he knows she's even there, or cares. It's not my business, but I have no idea why she's with a guy like that. Maybe she has low self-esteem or something. Not that I've cared about anyone or anything other than hockey for a long time now, and hey, who am I to judge anyone? I'm a total fuck-up.

"Kai," Bree whispers, and it pulls me from my reverie. I'm two seconds from walking away, but go still when skittish blue eyes lift and lock on mine. I stare back, my heart beating just a bit faster as Theo's girlfriend holds my gaze.

Why the fuck is she looking at me with such vulnerability? Oh wait, I get it. Theo isn't paying her attention and maybe she's...shit, I'm not going down this road again. No way am I going to let her close so she can make her man jealous.

"Go on, run inside," Theo laughs.

Don't engage, Kai. Don't fucking engage.

"I think I'll have another smoke," he taunts. "I don't even need to stretch out to beat you at scoring in tonight's game," he adds and something inside me snaps.

I stop, and the girls around me suck in a breath. Hands tug at me but I ignore them. "Yeah, want to bet?" I ask through clenched teeth.

What the hell are you doing dude?

"Bet?" he asks, his mouth twisted in a self-assured grin, but there's a hint of uncertainty in his eyes and I'm going to delve into that—because yeah, I'm that much of a prick. "Why would I bet on anything with you?"

I shrug, and press, "If you're so sure, let's put down a bet."

He snorts and glances at his friends, looking for their support and they give it. "Why would I bet when I know it's a sure thing?"

"Yeah, Ward. Why would he bet anything?" Kingston's right winger asks as he gives Theo a fist bump. Idiots.

Since this is getting tiring and I have a game to win, I point out, "Sounds to me like you're not so sure."

He drops his cigarette and stomps it out, dragging his arm away from his girlfriend so hard, she practically falls, which, for some odd reason that I don't understand, really pisses me off.

"What do you have to bet with, Ward? What could you possibly have that I want?" he asks and glances around at the cars in the lot. "You gonna put up the car you killed your buddy in?"

My heart stalls in my chest, and my throat squeezes so tight, I'm not sure I can get any air. A burst of sadness and shame invades my soul, and nearly weakens my knees, but anger that Theo could be so cold and crass overrules all other emotions and my hands fist as Bree's small palm lands on my back. Her small gasp doesn't go unnoticed.

"You know that car was totaled," I say through gritted teeth and don't miss the hushed chatter between Bree and her friends. "I'll put up my jeep."

"Kai," Bree whispers. "What are you doing?"

I really don't know.

Theo takes a small step toward me. "I suppose you want my car?"

I've seen his stupid sports car with the loud muffler. What was it I once overheard in the sorority? The bigger and louder the muffler, the smaller and thinner the cock. That thought makes me laugh.

"Nope."

He cocks his head, puzzled. "What do you want then?"

My gaze leaves his and lands on his girlfriend. Her eyes go wide, like I'd just slapped her in the face. "Her," is all I say.

Theo's gaze goes from me, to his girl, back to me. "What the fuck?"

His girlfriend tugs on Theo's coat, but he ignores her. With my blood pumping fast, I cross my arms, widen my legs, and wait as he works those details out in his tiny brain.

"You want my girl?" he finally asks.

"Do you need me to talk slower, and use smaller sentences?"

Theo glares at me for a split second and then snorts out a laugh. "That's fucking crazy." His groupies start laughing with him, because of course they do. Do any of them have a thought of their own?

I hold my stance and using smaller sentences, add, "Mine. For one month."

Theo stops laughing and his goons follow suit. Silence fills the night. "You're out of your fucking mind, Ward."

Of that I have no doubt.

"Wait, unless there's something real between you two," I say and wave my hand back and forth between the two of them. "I wouldn't want to come between the two of you if you're exclusive."

"We're not," he blurts out, and my gaze cuts to his girl in time to see her shoulders curl into herself. Jesus Christ. How deep am I going to shove the knife, and what the fuck is driving me? "But that doesn't mean this isn't crazy," Theo adds.

I bend and pick up my hockey bag. "Yeah, that's what I thought."

Theo takes another step closer. "I'm not fucking scared of you, BM."

BM: Buddy murderer.

I turn away before I do something I might not be able to come back from. "Never said you were," I toss my bag over my shoulder and pull open the door, ready to walk away but his voice stops me.

"Fine, if you win, and you won't, you can have Jami."

Jami...

I angle my body and glance at Jami. It's hard to tell in the dark, but I'm pretty sure she's gone ghostly pale. She stumbles back a bit, and I resist the urge to bolt forward, throw my arms around her and hold her upright. Theo sure as shit isn't doing anything to help her. Regret instantly grips me. Why did I fucking drag her into this? The better question is, why do I care? Like I said, it's been a long-ass time since I felt anything other than pain and regret. The only thing driving me these days is making it to the NHL.

"For one month," I clarify.

"One month," he agrees.

"You and her...broken up. Over completely for one month."

"Yeah, broken up. For one month," he agrees, but then snorts. "Like you're ever going to score more than me, anyway."

"No contact with her."

"Fine."

"If you don't stick to the rules, I won't either."

"What the fuck is that supposed to mean?"

"It means, if you break the rules, I'd be free to show Jami how a real man treats his woman. Then who knows what would happen."

"Like I'm fucking worried."

Actually, he does look worried, which is strange, considering the way he treats her. Jami, having had no say in this, backs up a bit, and before I can tell her I don't want anything from her—and maybe apologize for being an asshole—the crowd swallows her whole. My gut squeezes tight. What the fuck am I doing? Honestly, I'm not exactly sure what drove me to involve her—it's not like taking her away from Theo will hurt him. He doesn't value her at all. But Jami doesn't have to worry about me. When I win tonight, I'll let her know she's off the hook, that I don't want anything from her.

I nod at Theo and step through the door, and the word asshole follows me in as he shouts to me. I ignore him and Bree and her friends go silent. I head straight for the locker room to gear up. What I'm doing isn't smart, and I'm sure I'll have some explaining to do to Bree. Right now, however, I have some goals to score.

Thirty minutes later, I'm standing at center ice, face to face with Theo as the ref holds the puck between us.

"Eyes on the puck, not the player," he warns, and the second he lets go of the puck, I get it on the end of my stick and pass. Theo shoulders me as he skates off, but I don't let it rattle me. I have a game to win.

Jared carries the puck down the ice while I reposition, he shoots it to Brennan, who takes a fast and early shot, but misses. Theo smirks at me, and that's when I feel eyes on me. I usually ignore those in the stands, but my gaze strays to Jami. Theo turns to see who I'm smiling at, and let's face it, I'm only smiling at her to piss him off. I don't want Jami. Even if she's watching me with an intensity that's sort of messing with me.

"Fuck you," Theo grunts.

"Think she will?" I ask, purposely being a crude bastard just to piss him off, and it works. Although it's a little surprising. I've seen the way he treats her. He's about to throw a punch when Brennan skates over to me to guide me away.

"You good?" he asks.

"Yup, let's beat these fuckers."

He pushes on my helmet. "That's the plan."

We get back into the game, and it goes fast. First period ends in a goal for Kingston—scored by a very smug Theo. Second period ends in a tie—our goal scored by me. Now here we are, the clock ticking down, with minutes left, and the puck is on the end of Brennan's blade. He's skating fast, and the defense are coming at him. I get myself open, and he makes a clean pass. I grab the puck, transfer my weight, twist my torso and take my slapshot. The red-light flashes and the buzzer sounds. I throw my arms up and cheers erupt as my teammates pile on.

But right now, it's Theo's face I want to see, and maybe even Jami's. But for different reasons. I don't want her mad at me. In fact, I might want the opposite, and yeah maybe Theo's right and I am fucking crazy. She's from the opposing team and nothing about us makes sense.

Twenty minutes later, we're all finishing up our showers, and the energy is high in the locker room. I'm putting on a happy show for my teammates, hiding the knot in my stomach. I'm sure soon enough, though, the bet I made will be all over campus, but someone else will do something stupid and this incident will be all forgotten, especially after I tell Jami I'm not going to go through with it.

Foregoing a coat, I shut my locker and start toward the doors. Brennan throws his arm around me. "What's going on with you and douche bag?"

I laugh at that. "Trust me. You don't want to know."

He eyes me and I love that he and the team always have my back. "You sure?"

"Yeah, it's all under control," I assure him and hope I'm right.

His gaze moves over my face, and he finally gives in and says, "Okay, let's go get a drink."

"Make it two." It's Friday. I don't have classes tomorrow and I could use a cold one.

Outside, the cool night air falls over us and I spot Bree and her friends waiting. She comes up to me, a nervousness about her and I get it. I have some explaining to do.

"Hey Bree, want a ride?" Brennan asks and turns so she can jump on his back.

"Sure," she says tearing her gaze from me, and I instantly search the parking lot for Jami, not at all expecting to see her. When I find her leaning against the brick building, all alone, watching me, my heart jumps a bit with excitement and that's just fucked up.

"I'll meet you guys there," I say and Bree frowns at me before I take off. I jog over to where Jami is standing, and she folds her arms across her body, in a defensive move and it once again reminds me I pulled a prick move.

"Hey," I say, and put my hand on the wall next to her head. I lean in a bit and try not to notice the sweet, smell of her hair. "You don't have to do this. I shouldn't have—"

"Kai." She cuts me off, lifting her chin an inch. Her boldness shocks me. "I know you have an agenda of your own. Otherwise, you wouldn't have asked for me in this ridiculous bet." She pushes off the wall, her eyes uncertain but the determination that lives just behind that tentativeness intrigues me. "Maybe I have an agenda too."

"What's that supposed to mean?"

She reaches for my hand and the second my palm connects with her soft skin, the world goes a little wobbly around me. Her eyes hold mine and with a lift of her chin, she says, "We're doing this."

JAMI

I stare up at Kai, his hand wrapped around mine and I'm about to pull away, because yeah, this is a stupid mistake. I thought I could use him the way he was using me, and somehow make Theo jealous. Maybe then he'd realize I was a good girlfriend, always standing by his side, and just maybe, he'd appreciate me—see that I have worth.

But do you, Jami?

I'm about to run, to go bury my head under my blankets, when his big, warm hand tightens around mine, swallowing it entirely, and oddly enough, giving me a strange sense of comfort and security. Then again, what would I know about comfort and security? Okay, that's not entirely true. I was raised in a good family and had everything I needed, even if I was born because my brother needed a bone marrow transplant.

Spare.

God, I hate that term. But I sure as hell know how a certain royal feels when he says it.

"Are you sure you want to do this?" he asks, as those dark, intense eyes that exude pain roam over my face.

"Positive," I answer with more conviction than I really feel. Am I really going to be this guy's girlfriend for one month? He gives my hand a tug to set me into motion and I take a step with him.

Okay, apparently I am.

He pulls me close as someone comes our way on the sidewalk, and my body bumps his. I'm about to right myself, but he puts his arm around me and I instantly stiffen.

"Sorry," he blurts out quickly. "I thought..."

"It's okay. You just took me by surprise. I mean, I didn't expect..." He frowns, and pulls his arm away, and for the briefest of seconds I miss his warmth, and to be honest, I'm surprised he's warm. The night air is cool and he doesn't have a jacket.

He holds his hands up. "Won't happen again."

"Some boyfriend you are," I joke but it doesn't pull a laugh from him. In fact, he goes quiet. But I actually liked his arm around me, which just goes to show how starved I am for Theo's affection. I actually hate myself for how hard I try. Don't get me wrong, there are times Theo is really sweet and attentive. It's just that those times are few and far between these days. I realize he's trying hard to get to the NHL, but tonight, did he really need to pick a fight with Kai? Some of the things he said were cruel, to be honest. I don't know their history, though, but I don't think anyone should be that mean.

I vaguely remember there was an accident in the valley years ago. I was pretty sheltered, and I don't know much, other than a car went off the road in a snowstorm. Someone died, but no charges were laid. I don't know much more than that. Like I said, I was sheltered.

We walk in awkward silence for a minute, and he keeps casting me glances. I really don't want him to ask me about my personal agenda in all this foolishness. I'm not about to tell him. I probably never will. It's a bit embarrassing, really. Shouldn't my boyfriend want to make me feel important and special?

Maybe you should leave Theo and find someone who does treat you special, Jami.

Cripes, as a psychology student working toward a social work degree, I understand the four attachment styles and how they affect relationships, but I can't help wanting to be valued. The only problem is, a part of me just doesn't believe I have any value outside of being born to save my brother. My parents still shelter me. Probably fearing I'll get hurt and won't be around if my brother needs me again. My entire body stiffens. Kai must sense it as hesitation, because he abruptly stops walking.

He turns to me. "Listen, if you've changed your mind, if you want out, it's okay."

"No, I haven't and I don't," I assure him quickly. I blink rapidly. That's when it hits me. Maybe he really doesn't want to do this. "I'm sorry." I give a fast shake of my head. "Of course. You don't want to do this." God, why would he want me hanging around, and keeping him from the women he really wants to be with?

There's a moment of hesitation as his brow pulls together and then, he says, "I want to do this."

I continue to stare at him, and I'm not sure I ever realized just how handsome he is, with his dark intense eyes that look at me, and not through me. That small scar above his right eye does nothing to diminish his good looks. Add in a mess of brown curls, a square chin that has a scruff of a beard, and he has a whole ruggedness going on for him. Then again, maybe he doesn't care about anyone or anything other than himself. At least that's what Theo said in the past when he was trash talking about him.

Didn't he just ask you if you wanted out?

That must mean a part of him, even if it's deep inside, cares about others. Or at least he has a conscience beneath all that brawn and gruff.

"We normally head to the pub after a game. Do you want to go or do you want me to take you home?"

It's odd, but I sort of like this awkwardness about him. I've seen him around before. Plenty of times. Let's face it. He's hard to miss. The guys on our team often talk about him, too. Theo and Kai have been rivals for years. Like Theo, Kai exudes confidence and I've never seen him waver. He's wavering now, and I guess I like it because it makes him more human than godlike—the way everyone treats Theo.

"If I'm your girlfriend, I guess I should be doing girlfriend things with you and that includes celebrating your win and all that comes with it."

He snorts under his breath. "Yeah, you don't want to be doing all that comes with it."

Heat runs over my face. Okay, I get it. He's talking about sex. "No, you're right," I clarify. I don't want him to think I'm going to sleep with him. I have zero intentions of doing that.

First, I'm not a cheater—then again, I'm officially broken up with Theo—and second, my agenda is to hang with him with the hope that it triggers something in Theo, since all I want is to be seen, and third, I'm not attracted to him.

Hahahahahaha...

I shut down my stupid inner voice that is laughing hysterically at that third point. Fine, I admit he's good looking. I already said he was but he's not my type.

That's right, Jami. You like men who treat you like a commodity and pay you attention only when they feel like it.

The psychology student in me wants to pound some sense into my brain, but the truth is, I'm hoping after this stunt, Theo will see me differently. Maybe he'll realize that while he says we're not exclusive, neither one of us have been seeing anyone else for months now. Lots of guys are terrified of commitment, and maybe it's foolish of me to think this will help him overcome it, but I have to try something.

"Let's go then." We start walking and his body is so big next to mine. Every now and then he moves closer to let someone pass on the sidewalk and always apologizes if he bumps me. It's kind of sweet.

I steal a glance at his profile. "Are your friends going to hate me?" I ask, my stomach tightening.

He gives a fast shake of his head. "No, why?"

"I am the enemy, Kai," I remind him with a chuckle that holds no humor. Truthfully, I don't have many friends of my own, and I might have been a bit envious of his circle of friends. I only have my classmates, and my roommate, and we're not close. We simply have college in common. I don't party much, never have, and on the weekends, I go home to

Greenwood, about two hours away, to work in the military family resource center. When I complete my studies, I want to work in the family resource center, on base.

Up ahead, I spot the girl he was with earlier. She might be getting a piggyback ride from one of Kai's teammates, but I don't miss the way she keeps glancing back to check on Kai. "Is she...your girlfriend?" I ask, and Kai glances at me.

"Who?"

I gesture up ahead and he follows my gaze. "You mean Bree?" As he looks at me like I might have been dropped on my head at birth, I nod and a strange snorting sound rises in his throat. "No," he says quickly. "I don't have a girlfriend."

Duly noted, especially the aversion in his voice when he used the word girlfriend. Okay, he's single and plans to stay that way, and I'm not the one who's going to break it to him that Bree would like to be his girlfriend. That's his business, not mine, and if he can't see it, that's on him. I don't want Bree to hate me though. She actually seems really sweet. So do her friends. I love how they tried to pull Kai away from Theo when things were heating up.

My steps slow a bit, and as if sensing my sudden hesitancy, he takes my hand in his. "We don't—"

"You're going to tell your friends nothing about this is real, right?"

"You mean the guys I play with, and the cheerleaders and puck bunnies?"

Okay that is a strange thing to say. Does he not consider them his friends? "Yeah, those friends." He shakes his head like I have it wrong, so I say, "I guess Bree probably filled everyone in."

"Yeah I'm sure. Not to gossip or anything, but she would have given them the heads up. They all would have found it odd to see me walking in with you."

"Because I'm from the rival team?"

"Because you're a girl," he clarifies.

"And you don't like girls?"

He laughs. "No, it's not that."

He leaves it at that as we reach the pub, and I glance up as noise spills from the open windows. This is all strange to me. I'm not used to going out with the team after a game, win or loss. Theo always told me it was time for him to be with his teammates and I understood that.

Kai pushes open the heavy door and cheers erupt as he enter. I spot his friends seated around a huge table, and the drinks are flowing freely. I move closer to Kai, totally out of my element, and he gives me a glance, like he's checking in with me. I nod, and he nods back and the next thing I know, his friends are squishing together to make room for us at the table.

I catch Bree's eye and she gives me a smile, but it's shaky. I smile back as two mugs are placed in front of us and drinks are poured.

"You look familiar," Bree says to me.

"Maybe you know me from the games," I say loudly, over the noise as my gaze moves over her pretty face. "Actually, you look familiar too." Now that I really see her, I think we might have met. "Have I seen your around Kingston campus? Were we in a class together."

"No, I go to Scotia Academy. I'm a design student. I work at Coffee Culture," she tells me. "Maybe we know each other from there."

That's when it hits me. "Ohmigod, you're the one who gave me the free coffee. Remember that time I had a dentist appointment and my face was swollen and I couldn't find my wallet."

She laughs. "Sorry, not laughing at your predicament, but yes, I remember now. You looked like you were about to cry and I just wanted to put a smile on your swollen face."

I laugh at that. "You were so incredibly sweet. I owe you a coffee."

"No, you don't owe me anything." Her gaze slides to Kai. "Just watch out for him, okay?"

"I will," I say and want to tell her it's okay. Nothing is ever going to happen between Kai and me and her concern is sweet. She obviously knows him well, and it's sort of hard to believe he described her as a girl he knows.

Kai nudges me, and lifts his glass. I do the same and everyone else does as well. "To kicking ass tonight," someone says and we all do a salute, and just when I expect to shrink into myself, much like I do with Theo, and let the night play out around me, Kai speaks up.

"Hey guys, this is Jami." He glances at me with those rich eyes of his, and something about his demeanor puts me at ease and I sit up a bit straighter. "I'm sure you all know what went down before the game."

"Yeah man, we heard," one of his teammates says. "Bree filled us in."

I catch Bree's glance and I'm guessing she didn't fill them in on everything, like when Theo said something about the car that killed Kai's buddy. Theo also called him BM, although I have no idea what that means, and from the rage it roused in Kai's eyes, I have no intentions of asking.

"So, for the next bit, Jami is going to be hanging out with us, and I don't need to say this, but I will anyway." I swallow and brace myself, having no idea what's going to come out of his mouth. "You're all going to treat her like she's one of ours."

"Yeah man," one of the other guys says and glasses are lifted in a salute again. "Of course, we are."

"Jami," he begins and starts introducing me to those around the table. Not that I'll remember their names but it's kind of nice that he's bothering to do it at all. After an exchange of pleasantries, I sip on my beer, and for the first time in a long time, I'm actually relaxed and enjoying myself. Beside me, Kai laughs at a joke his friend Mason just blurted out and I try not to notice the way Kai's leg presses against mine with each loud rumble.

Two big trays of nachos are set on the table, and everyone digs in. I sit back, and Kai pulls the biggest cheesiest nacho from the center of the pile, but instead of eating it, he holds it in front of my mouth.

"Open," he commands in a soft tone, and I have no idea what's going on, but for some reason the deepness in his voice, combined with his suddenly possessive tone does strange things to me.

I open my mouth and he places the cheesy nachos on my tongue. "Omigod, so delicious," I moan and reach for a napkin to wipe the salsa that spilled on my chin, suddenly wondering if I have some weird fetish about being fed.

"Best in the city," he tells me. "What, you've never had nachos here before?"

"I've never been in this pub before," I tell him.

"Right, rival teams." He gives me a wink and I nod in agreement, even though it's not entirely true. I don't much enjoy eating alone and I'd be hard pressed to find a friend to call to join me. I don't really fit into many groups. He leans into me and his breath is warm on my cheek. "We're a team now, Jami."

I work to ignore the quickening of my pulse as his body crowd's mine. "For a month, anyway," I remind him, and his body goes rigid, the muscles along his jaw hardening before my eyes.

"Hey, Jami," Brennan calls. At least I think his name is Brennan. I turn to him, and raise a brow.

"Are you coming to the fundraiser tomorrow?" He glances at Kai.

I look at Kai. "I...I don't know."

"The team and a few others raise money for the local children's hospital," Kai explains.

"I usually go home to Greenwood on the weekends. I volunteer at the military family center," I tell him. "But if it's for the children." I kind of like that his team works with the children's hospital. Theo's team doesn't do anything like that.

Kai shifts in his seat, and puts his mouth near my ear. "You don't have to come if you don't want to, Jami."

Maybe he doesn't want me to go. It was his friend who brought it up, after all. I eye him as he inches back and I say,

"Supporting a team is what a girlfriend would do though, right?"

He shrugs. "Sure, as long as you don't mind getting wet."

"I'm not made of sugar," I tell him, only for his gaze to drop and focus on my lips. I lick them in response and add, "I don't mind getting wet."

Wait, did he just gulp?

3

KAI

I lay in bed, my room pitch black, and go over the events of the night. Usually, I'm worn out after a game and a couple beers and fall right to sleep. Tonight however, I can't slow my brain down. Did I really win Jami in a bet? Jesus, what was I thinking?

While I feel bad that I treated her like a commodity, and that her asshole boyfriend agreed, I'm at least glad she has an agenda of her own and isn't going along with this because she feels she has to. I suspect she's trying to make Theo jealous. Much like his girlfriend did back in high school. Why can't they see that he's not worth the effort? Hell, if Jami was my girl, though that's never going to happen because I have zero plans to get serious with anyone, I'd never thrust her into the arms of another man.

My room suddenly lightens up and I turn toward my phone on my nightstand. My heart jumps. Could it be Jami? We exchanged numbers after I saw her home safely, but what reason would she have to message me? I reach for my phone and see that it's Bree, asking how I'm doing. My chest tightens. We didn't talk after the game, and I'm sure she has questions. I message back that I'm good and I'll see her tomorrow at the car wash. I wait for a response and when none comes, I run my finger over my phone and stare at Jami's contact information. I have no reason to message her either, but oddly enough, I want to.

Don't do it, dude.

Ignoring that wise inner voice, something I don't normally do, a bout of guilt for this whole bet hits as I shoot off a message to Jami.

Me: Hey...

Wow, what a wordsmith. Maybe I should become a writer like Brandon Cannon, a former player on my team, or even Jemma, my buddy Kace Andrew's wife. Kace plays for Edmonton now and if I had the choice, that'd be the NHL team I'd want to play for. I'm about to set my phone down. Why would Jami respond to 'hey', but stop when three dots appear. No freaking way, but more importantly, why is my damn heart racing?

Jami: Hey back at you. Can't sleep?

Me: Thinking about tomorrow.

Not a lie. I am thinking about tomorrow. The yearly fundraiser is always a lot of fun, and I hope Jami enjoys it. I know everyone will treat her right. That doesn't mean I'm going to leave her side. I won her in a bet, and to me, that makes her my responsibility. Which again makes me wonder what the fuck I was thinking. After I've kept my distance. The last thing I'd ever want is to hurt someone I care about, which is why I refuse to care.

Jami: ...

Jami: If you don't want me there.

Me: No, that's not it. I don't want to keep you from going back home.

Jami: It's okay. I can get someone to cover for me, or I can always drive down after the car wash. I volunteer for the youth dances at the military family resource center.

Me: Sounds fun.

Jami: Come with.

My heart jumps. Is she serious? After the car wash, I don't really have anything keeping me in the city. I could always head home and see if my parents need any help in the vineyard, I suppose. It's harvest time, and I actually enjoy the whole process.

Me: Okay.

Jami: ...

As I stare at the phone, I get the feeling that she didn't expect me to agree. Is she going to tell me she was kidding?

Jami: Great. We can leave early afternoon. Actually, I'm glad you messaged.

Once again, my stupid heart jumps. Is she happy to hear from me? Okay, I don't want that. I don't want her to think I bet on her because I liked her. No, she's smart. She so much as told me she knew I had an agenda.

Me: What's up?

Jami: How do you like your coffee?

Me: Why?

Jami: Curious.

Me: Lots of sugar.

Jami: You like sweet, huh?

I pinch my eyes shut and try not to think about earlier, when she told me she wasn't made of sugar and didn't mind getting wet. Jesus, those lips of hers. So lush and inviting. I nearly got a hard-on when she licked them. Honestly, she might not be made of sugar, but I bet she tastes as sweet. *Do NOT go down that road, Kai.* This time, I do listen to that voice. I am not going to lay a fucking finger on my rival's girlfriend. Or rather ex-girlfriend, which means... No. No. No. I continue to repeat that mantra as I message back.

Me: Yeah.

Jami: Okay, see you in the morning.

Me: Later, Jami.

I stare at the phone and when no more messages come in, I set it down, roll on my side and stare at it until it goes dark. Why the hell am I smiling like the goddamn village idiot? I immediately wipe the smile from my face and kick off the blankets as darkness envelops me again. The cool night air chills my skin and I let it. Sometimes—all the time—I don't think I deserve all the comforts I have.

I hug myself thinking about blue eyes and soft lips and the next thing I know, the sun is shining in my room, and I open my eyes to find my blankets up around my shoulders. I obviously pulled them up in my sleep. I kick them off and turn toward my phone. I check it for messages and go through my emails. For the briefest of seconds, I think about checking Jami's socials, only to realize I don't know her last name.

I hear my roommate Thomas banging around in the hall before the shower turns on and my stomach grumbles. I push from my bed, stumble over my clothes on the floor, and dressed only in my boxers, I head downstairs to the kitchen. The second I shove a pod in the coffee maker, my mind goes to Jami. Okay, who am I kidding? She was the last thing I thought about before I fell sleep and the first thing I thought about this morning, which makes me want to end this whole ridiculous arrangement.

Yeah, that's what I'm going to do. As soon as I see her, I'm going to tell her this bet is off and I won't be going with her to the valley after the car wash. This is all so fucking stupid. I grumble under my breath and stare at my cup until it fills with coffee. I toss in three cubes of sugar—again trying not to think of Jami—and take a much-needed sip. I turn, lean against the counter, and just sip my coffee until Thomas comes into the kitchen, dressed in sweats as he rubs a towel in his hair.

"Coffee?" I ask.

"Yeah, definitely."

I throw another pod in the machine as he opens the fridge. He grabs the eggs. "So, you and Jami Nichols, huh."

Nichols. Ah, that's her last name.

He gives a low slow whistle. "What?" I ask.

"You seem like an odd couple."

That's when I remember Thomas went to school in Greenwood and was my rival until we were both recruited by Scotia Academy. Who knew I could end up roommates with a guy I played against my whole life?

"We're not a couple. You know what's going on." His coffee beeps and I hand it to him. "How well do you know her?"

He smirks at me. "If you're not a couple, why the sudden interest?"

"Fuck off," I snap and he laughs.

He shrugs. "She's quiet, actually. She spent a lot of time with her older brother as far as I remember. They were close. I have no idea how she ended up with a loudmouth like Theo."

"You know him well?"

"Unfortunately." I take it Thomas doesn't much care for Theo either.

"Did you know her brother? I don't remember him. I don't remember playing against him in any sports."

"He missed a lot of school from what I can remember."

I nod, and finish my coffee as Thomas' cat comes sauntering into the kitchen. "I wonder what that was all about."

"Not sure." He picks up Mittens, and starts petting him. He found the cat under the house when we moved in and because he has white on his paws, he called him Mittens. "He graduated before me, and I really don't know any more than that."

I set my cup in the sink as Thomas puts Mittens back down and sets a frying pan on the stove. "I need a shower."

He goes to work on breakfast and I grab a quick shower. Once done, I dress in jeans and a T-shirt and head back down to find a plate of eggs on the table for me. I always tell Thomas not to cook for me, but he does it anyway. We're roommates but I don't want him to think we're buddies.

I grab the ketchup, and cover my eggs, which always disgusts Thomas, but he's not in the kitchen to complain. After I eat,

I check my phone again, and try to curb the disappointment in my gut when there are no messages from Jami.

Jami Nichols.

She's my enemy's girlfriend and not someone I should be hanging out with. Which is why I'm going to end this the second I see her. I could do it with a text, but even I'm not that much of a prick, and to be honest, she actually seemed stoked about helping out today. She must really like kids.

"Ready?" Thomas asks from the doorway as I load the dishwasher.

"Two seconds." I hurry upstairs to brush my teeth and toss a change of clothes into my bag. Downstairs, I follow Thomas outside, and I'm pleasantly surprised to find it's bright and warm. We'll get much more business on a sunny day.

Since the service station that's hosting us is only a few blocks away, we walk there and as we approach, a nervous knot tightens in my stomach. Maybe Jami will come to her senses too, and not show up. I scan the crowd gathering, and breathe a sigh when Jami is nowhere to be found.

"You good, bud?" Thomas asks as Brennan comes running to catch up to us. He jumps on my back, and he's so goddamn big and heavy my legs nearly give.

"What the fuck, dude?" I groan as he jumps off and laughs.

"Hey, so what's Bree's story anyway?" I turn and catch the interest in his eyes.

"I don't think she has a story."

"Is she seeing anyone?" I shrug. "You two are friends, aren't you?"

"I know her."

Brennan and Thomas exchange a look before Brennan curses. "Jesus." I narrow my eyes and he gives a frustrated shake of his head. "What I'm asking is if you're interested in her. You know, as more than a friend." I'm about to correct him that we're not friends, but he cuts me off by saying, "You guys are always hanging out."

"No, we're..." I stop myself from calling her my friend. "We know each other. If you like her, go for it." Bree and Brennan. Hmph. I don't think I saw that coming. Wait, why does everyone think I like Bree? Jami asked about her too. I mean, I do like her. She's nice. But I don't want her to be my girlfriend. I don't want a girlfriend.

Car horns honk as a few of the cheerleaders hold up signs, inviting the drivers to have their cars cleaned. Music blares louder as we get closer, and I walk over to Cameron's SUV and drop my bag into the back to keep it dry.

"Hey," Bree calls out when she sees me and threatens to aim the hose my way. I laugh and step up to her.

"Give me that," I say and take it from her. A bunch of the girls who always hang with us after a game continue to wash the car, and I wipe my brow as the late morning sun shines down on me. I can't help but glance around.

"Maybe she's not coming?" Bree says quietly.

"Who?"

"Your girlfriend."

"You know she's not my girlfriend. I don't want a girlfriend."

She glances down and squeezes soap out of her sponge, and it spills onto the ground. "I know."

"Hey, who's in need of coffee?" I glance up quickly and spot Jami coming our way. A tray of coffees in each hand. My heart thumps. She searches the crowd and catches my gaze, giving me a little smile. The guys start pulling the paper cups from the tray. "Don't worry, I have more. There's cappuccino, americano, drip and don't touch that one," she says as Mason tries to grab one. "That's extra sweet for Kai."

Aww, Jesus.

She hands a coffee to Bree. "I owe you this."

"You don't owe me anything, but thank you. This was very sweet."

She holds the tray out to me, one cup left. "What are you doing?" I ask.

"Bringing everyone coffee. I thought we could all use something strong after last night." I stand there in awe of her. Well fuck.

"Hey where's mine?" Trey asks.

"Don't worry. I have more trays in the back of my car."

"Omigod, this is delicious," Bree moans.

Jami chuckles. "I had a feeling you were a pumpkin latte kind of girl."

Bree's eyes light up. "How did you know that?"

"It's my favorite too, and I have a feeling we like the same things." Her gaze slowly moves to mine. What the hell? Is she talking about me? "I'll be right back."

"I can help," Bree says and as the two walk away, I can't help but think Jami could use a friend like Bree. I take a sip of my coffee. Jesus, that's delicious. I look at the cup and read the label. I never heard of Kellan's before. Is it some local coffee shop I know nothing about. I'll have to rectify that.

"Do you have a flat white?" Brad asks.

"I do." She checks the cups and pulls one from the tray. "You're Brad, right?" he nods. "Kellan told me to give this to someone named Brad."

Brad grins. "That's me. How do you know Kellan?"

"He's my brother."

"Oh, wow I had no idea." Brad flicks the tab on the lid, takes a drink and moans. "He makes the best coffee in town."

"Kai," someone says and I turn to see Lucy pointing to the car, her white shirt completely soaked. Yeah, okay, that's going to bring in business. Oddly enough, I kind of hope Jami doesn't do that. "We need a spray," she tells me as she flicks her wet hair from her face. I aim my hose at the car, my focus still on Jami and Bree as they both come back with trays of gourmet coffee.

Okay dude, you need to end this now.

Jami and Bree hand out the coffees and go back for more. How many did she bring? Now she's even handing them to driver's waiting in line for the car wash. I shake my head at her generosity.

She finally finishes and steps up to me. "Now what can I do?"

"Where's your coffee?" I ask.

She crinkles her nose. "Oh, I didn't keep one for myself. I didn't want anyone to miss out."

I swallow against a suddenly tight throat. I hold my cup out. "Have some of mine." She glances at my outstretched arm and hesitates. "Unless you don't like sweet?"

"No, I do."

"Then you're afraid of my cooties?" I blurt out and she laughs at that. "That's it isn't it?" I nudge her. "You think I have cooties?"

Her eyes light up as she laughs. "No, I don't think—"

"Well, I don't have anything to be afraid of." Before I can stop myself or think better of it, I lean in and press my lips to hers. As the warmth of her soft lips seep through my body, her gasp fills the air and falls around me. I pull back and my heart thunders.

What the fuck.

Okay, I really shouldn't have done that, and I definitely need to put an end to this charade. I am not going down that road, or any road with her. But wait, she shut her eyes when I kissed her and they're still closed. Not to mention the way she's leaning toward me, her lips still puckered. Did she...like it?

Before I can speak, her lids fly open and she straightens, pulling herself together much faster than I do. She takes the cup—like nothing at all transpired between us—lifts it in salute and says, "It was never about the cooties. I just wanted you to enjoy a whole cup." This girl is just too fucking good to be true. Yeah, I think she is, which is all the more reason I need to keep my distance. She takes a sip and the resulting moan rising in her throat wraps around my cock and tugs. "So good," she murmurs, her eyes closing.

Okay, time to end this...now.

"Uh, Jami." She blinks her eyes open and hands the cup back to me. Our fingers touch and little sparks zip through me.

"Yes?"

I stare at her big blue eyes, take in the warmth and vulnerability, her gentle kindness. "I was thinking…I mean…I was uh, just wondering." She angles her head and watches me intently, and that's when something in me gives and I continue with, "Where did you get this coffee?"

Jesus, Kai.

JAMI

I cast Kai a glance as I use a sponge to soap up the last car in the line, and by this point, my shorts and T-shirt are pretty soaked. At least I'm not wearing white, and I don't really mind getting wet when it's this unseasonably warm out. I'm actually having a good time, and his friends have all been very nice to me. I suppose he warned them, and I don't think Kai is a guy anyone wants to mess with.

Do not think about messing with Kai, Jami.

How can I not after that kiss? It was fast, but so damn hot and sweet...and I'd be lying if I said I didn't want it to last just a little bit longer, which is absolutely insane. I'm not with Kai for love and affection. We both have our own agendas. But holy hell, I have no idea how I pulled myself together so quickly after his lips touched mine. It's been pure torture being around him ever since. Honestly, I still can't understand why he did it. Was it to prove he didn't have cooties, or...did he want to? Maybe I don't want to delve into that any deeper.

Last night after Kai and I texted, Theo reached out to me. He whined about me going off with Kai to the pub—I honestly didn't even think he knew, as I always go home after the games—but he was the one who treated me like a commodity. I'm only going along with this farce to see where this takes my relationship with Theo. I can only hope it smartens him up and he sees that I've been a great girlfriend. Although last night's texts really were all about him. He didn't ask how I felt, how my night went, or even if I got home safely. Then again, why would he ask if I got home okay after the game. He never has before.

Maybe you really are nothing but a commodity, Jami.

"You okay?" Kai asks, as I pull my shirt away from my body.

I swallow against the tightness in my throat. "Yup," I assure him and plaster on a happy face. "I'll definitely have to get changed before we head to the valley."

He takes a drink of water from a bottle. "I could really use another cup of coffee. I'm going to have to check out your brother's restaurant. I never heard of it before."

"It's just up on Spring Garden Road. It's fairly new. I'm probably going to stop in there before leaving the city. You want to come check it out?"

"Yeah, sure. Must be nice to have a chef in the family."

I put my hand on my stomach. "Maybe too nice," I laugh.

He laughs with me as I stick out my belly. "I never knew your brother. I think he was a couple grades ahead of me so we never played any sports against each other."

"Yeah, he's a bit older," I tell him. What I don't tell him is there's a big gap in our ages because I was only born to save him. No one needs that sob story and honestly, I love my brother dearly, and would do anything for him. "You'll like him."

He scratches his head and frowns. "Kellan Nichols. Did he play hockey?"

"No," is all I say. My parents basically kept him in a bubble after his childhood illness. When he wanted to become a chef, they nearly lost their minds. Apparently, they were worried about him working with sharp objects. I kind of feel sorry for Kellan, with all the helicopter parenting. Then again, I was subjected to it too. "I actually wanted to play."

"Really?"

"You seemed surprised."

"I don't know why. I know lots of women who play hockey. Why didn't you?"

"My parents thought it was too dangerous. I think they'd still have me in bubble wrap if they could." That brings a laugh. "I curl, though. A lot safer."

"I don't know much about it."

"Come watch me sometime." I don't really know why I suggested that. Of course, he's not going to watch me curl and he'd probably be bored out of his mind if he did.

"Love to." I glance at him, expecting to see that he's joking, but he's not. He's probably just a good actor, because no way is he going to show. "Why curling?"

"I was late signing up. I actually wanted archery. I thought it would be fun to do competitive archery."

His brow raises. "That's a bit dangerous, isn't it?"

I shrug. "Only if you're on the other end of the arrow."

"Note to self." He holds a finger up. "Do not stand on the other end of Jami's arrow."

I dip my sponge into the soapy bucket. "Competitive axe throwing was full too."

He laughs and holds up another finger. "Second note to self. Keep Jami away from the axe." I grin. "You have a bit of a wild streak in you, Nichols."

I put my fingers to my lips. "Shh, that's our secret." His grin widens and there's just something fun in having a secret with him. Although it's not really a secret. I just wouldn't want a lecture from my parents if they found out.

"Okay, that's a wrap," Jacob, the team captain, says, and when I see everyone throw their sponges up in the air, I do the same. It lands with a splat, and I yelp and jump back. Which is ridiculous, as I'm already soaked. Come to think of it, Kai looks like he's the only one whose still dry. That gives me an idea.

I wiggle my fingers at him. "Pass me the hose, I'm going to roll it up," I say casually. He looks like he's about to protest, and I continue, "Would you mind rinsing the soap from my sponge. You're stronger, you'll get more water out." He looks a bit skeptical as he hands the hose over, and bends to grab the sponge. That's when I turn the hose on him.

He yelps and squeals and everyone laughs as I turn the spray up and really drench him. "Jami," he yells. "You're going to pay for that."

Bree comes up beside me, along with her friends, and they're all jumping and laughing as Kai holds his hands out trying to stop the spray and she closes the distance between us.

"You are in so much trouble," Bree warns with a laugh and that's when Brennan takes the hose from me. "Run," he warns, and I'm laughing so hard I can barely put one foot in front of the other. I turn back and watch Kai wrestle the hose from Brennan and when he gets it, he drops it, zeroes in on me and starts running.

I squeal, but I have nowhere to hide, and there is no way I can outrun a powerful hockey player like Kai. Big arms wrap around me from behind and pick me clear up off my feet. "Put me down," I yell and wiggle but he's too strong.

"Why would you do that?" he asks, but there's a playfulness about him.

"You were the only dry one. I thought you should be wet too."

He groans in my ear, walks me back to his friends who are still laughing. "Bree, hand me the hose."

"No," I scream, even though I don't think he's going to turn that cold water on me. But I don't really know him so it's possible.

"No way," she says and holds it behind her. Her friend grabs it and runs away with it.

"You're all siding with Jami?" he asks, incredulous. He sets me down but doesn't let go of me. "Is it because of the coffee?"

"That didn't hurt," Summer admits.

He scoffs. "Are you guys that easily bought?"

"Apparently," Jacob laughs, coming up and slapping Brennan on the shoulder. "Great work today, everyone. Beers at the pub?"

I grumble under my breath. "Can't. Gotta bounce."

"Bree, you coming?" Brennan asks her and she tears her gaze away from Kai. My stomach clenches. Kai really has no idea how much she likes him, but she doesn't have to worry about me. Even if I was single and attracted to him, I'd never do anything to come between the two of them. I think it's only a matter of time before Kai figures out what a great girl she is.

"Are you mad?" I ask as I turn to him.

"No, but payback is a bitch," he teases and I laugh. When was the last time I laughed so hard?

He peels off his wet t-shirt and that's when I hear a strange, garbled noise in my ears. I glance around to see who made it, only to realize it was me, and yes, from the smirk on Kai's face, he heard it too. Ugh.

"So uncomfortable," I say quickly to cover my moan of appreciation as I tug at my shirt. "Unlike you, I can't just tug it off."

"You can, you just shouldn't," he laughs. "Come on, let's get you home and into some dry clothes. I actually have a bag packed. I didn't know if I'd be going out after the car wash or not."

He starts toward Cameron's SUV and grabs his duffle bag. "I have my car. Do you want me to drop you off at your place?"

"I can get changed at yours if it's easier."

"Either is fine, but no sense in making two stops, I guess. Unless you have to pack for the night."

"I still have a ton of clothes at home. I'm good."

"I'm here," I say, and wave toward my car. He hikes his bag up and follows me. "I'm going to get your seat all wet."

"I actually have some cardboard in the back. I used the crates to carry the coffee. Let's sit on those, otherwise it's going to be a long drive home on wet seats."

We reach my vehicle and I pop the hatch and he pulls out the cardboard boxes, breaking them down. "That was really nice of you to provide coffee."

"It wasn't completely altruistic," I tell him with a grin. "My brother is just getting started and I wanted to get everyone hooked on his coffee."

"You hooked me, that's for sure." After Kai breaks down one of the boxes he puts it on the driver's seat. "Is his food as good as his coffee?"

"Yeah, and you're going to find out today."

I nod. "I told him we were headed back home and he's making us a picnic lunch."

"Wow, where have you been my whole life?" We both laugh at that, because we both know it's a joke. He's not looking for a relationship and I'm in one. I realize for the next month, Theo and I are officially broken up, but the plan is to get back together, once he starts appreciating me.

"You good?" Kai asks, and he circles the car and puts carboard down on his seat.

"Yeah, just thinking."

"About your boyfriend?" he teases.

"Yes, I mean no. Who's my boyfriend?"

He laughs. "Apparently, I'm supposed to hold that title. You know, the bet." He climbs in. "Did you know Kace Andrews? He's gone off to the NHL to play for Edmonton."

I crinkle my nose. "I think I remember him. He was a center, and really fast."

"Yeah."

"He and his wife Jemma pretended to be a couple because there was a baby involved." My head rears back. I don't know anything about that. "It's complicated," he explains. "Anyway, my point is, they pretended and now they're married. Crazy, eh?"

"Did either of them have a boyfriend or girlfriend?"

"Not as far as I know."

I nod. "Then I guess I can see it happening. Our situation is different," I explain. Why the heck is he bringing this up? I narrow my eyes and assess his face as I start the car.

"Oh no, I'm not saying that's going to happen to us. Hell no." Okay, way to make your point clear. "I just thought it was funny. And don't worry. We're together because of a bet, and I don't want anything from you, Nichols."

"Good, because I don't want anything from you either, Ward." I go quiet for a moment. "I guess that's not entirely true."

"Oh."

I suppose there's really no harm in telling him. The truth is, we're not even friends. Heck, he doesn't even call his friends, friends. "I want to make Theo jealous," I admit and tug on my bottom lip with my teeth. Does that make me sound horrible? He goes quiet for a long time. "Kai."

His body shifts and he glances at me, an intense kind of serious about him. "It's your life and not my business. But shouldn't he already be jealous? Hell, if you were mine, I'd never agree to any kind of fucked up bet." I open my mouth and he holds his hands up. "Sorry, not my place. I just think you deserve better and that's all I'm going to say about Theo."

I nod and quietly ask, "What do you want out of this?"

His gaze holds mine and my pulse jumps. He, of course, isn't going to say *me,* because this isn't about me, and I don't expect that or want that, so it's odd that those are the words I want to hear on his tongue.

"I just wanted to put Theo in his place," I explain. Then he turns from me, leaving me with the sense there is more he wants to say but isn't going to. Maybe that's for the best. Maybe I don't want to hear what he thinks. "Do you hate me for that?"

"No," I assure him. "I don't hate you. I don't even know you, Kai." He nods in agreement, and that's when it occurs to me that maybe I would like to get to know him, even though that's probably not a good idea.

5

KAI

Okay, so apparently, I am going down this road with Jami Nichols. I roll my window down as Jami drives us through the city streets toward her place. I have no idea where she lives but I've become very familiar with the city after living here for three years.

I stretch my legs out. "I'm not used to being on this side of the vehicle," I tell her, lightening things between us after our somewhat uncomfortable conversation about Theo and our truth in what we both want out of this bet.

She casts me a quick glance and I admire her pretty blue eyes. "Do you hate it? Wait, are you the kind of guy who always has to be in charge?"

I take it she's familiar with those kinds of guys. I push back into my seat and wiggle a bit. "Actually, no. I could get used to being chauffeured around." The truth is, I don't much like driving anymore, and I really don't like having passengers. What if...

I stop myself, refusing to go there today.

She laughs at that. "I like to drive. It's my thinking time."

"What do you think about when you drive?" I ask her.

Her fingers tighten on the steering wheel, it's a slight movement but I notice it. She gives an easy shrug. "Lots of things."

"Okay, don't tell me then." I turn back to face the road.

She chuckles, even though I get the sense that her thoughts are dark and full of turmoil, much like mine. She flicks on her signal light and pulls into a driveway. Her residence is close to her college, naturally. I glance up and take in the big yellow house. Halifax isn't a big city, so I've seen it before. I'd just never been inside. I wince and hold my hand up to shade my eyes against the cheery sunshine yellow paint. "I should have worn sunglasses."

"I didn't choose the color," she explains, and winces with me. "It's horrible, I know."

"You can probably see this place from space."

"Funny you say that. When I was really young, I wanted to be an astronaut."

I shake my head, a little surprised at the things she's telling me. I expected her to be more of a closed book. "You're full of all kinds of surprises."

"I'm full of something," she murmurs under her breath and it makes me laugh.

I make a fist and nudge her chin. "You're all right, Nichols."

"Yeah, you're all right too, Ward, despite the fact that you pulled me into this ridiculous feud you have with Theo."

My heart sinks as she reaches for the door. "That was a prick move. I'm sorry. Like I said—"

She cuts me off. "Nope, we're seeing this thing through. We've come too far to back down now."

We've only been at it a day, and we could back out. But she's determined, and even though I was going to back out this morning before she showed up, what do I really have to lose?

Your focus, bro.

Right. I can't let anything veer me off track. I have to make the NHL, for Cooper's sake. I climb from the car, grabbing the damp cardboard from both seats as she snags my bag from the back. I take it from her and follow her to her front door.

"What made you change your mind?" I ask.

"I told you. Theo."

"No, I meant about being an astronaut." Dammit, every time she says his name it's like a punch to the nuts. How could he be so callous about my best friend's death, and to call me a BM. A shudder goes through me and I work to control it. "Too dangerous for your overprotective parents?"

"You got it," she tells me and before I can think better of it, I tap the center of her chest with my two fingers. Her eyes go wide and I pull my hand back.

"I was just going to say you have a lot of spirit." I glance at her chest. "In there. You're an adventurist at heart." I shift uncomfortably. "I bet you want to travel the world."

She unlocks the door and we step inside. "I do, although I don't see that happening." I don't miss the sudden sadness in her.

"Why not?"

"School, volunteering, work. I can barely keep afloat as it is. What about you? Do you want to travel?"

"I'll travel when I make the NHL."

She takes the cardboard from me. "That will be nice." I follow her to the kitchen where she puts the carboard into a compost bin. "Did you always want to play hockey?"

"Something like that." When I don't say more, she glances at me over her shoulder. She looks like she wants to ask something, so I hold my bag up to stop her before conversation takes me down a path I'd rather not revisit today. "Where can I get changed?"

"Top of the stairs, first left is my bedroom, but if you need a towel, you can change in the bathroom." She coughs, and puts her hand over her mouth. "Sorry, I have a tickle in my throat. Allergies. I wonder what's setting them off." She points. "Bathroom...second door on the left."

"Do you have a roommate?"

She wipes her hands on a piece of paper towel, and her brow lifts. "Yeah, why?"

I jerk my head toward the stairs at the front of the house. "Is she up there?"

She shakes her head as she coughs again and reaches for a glass. I step up to her, grab it and fill it with tap water. She graciously accepts and takes a big swallow.

"Thanks."

"Bad allergies, huh? You need to suck on something."

Jesus.

"I usually have some menthol cough drops. That always helps." She opens and closes a couple of drawers.

"Wait." I reach into my bag, only to pull out a package of cough drops with two left. I cringe as I peel the wrapper and find a gooey sugary mess.

"How long have they been in there?" she asks.

"Since my last cold."

"Twelve years ago?"

I chuckle. "Last year. It can't be that bad. It's not like they expire. They're basically sugar." I toss it into my mouth and she looks horrified. "Once you get past the liquified syrup, it's not too bad." She coughs again and I open the last one. "Open." She opens her mouth and I slide it in. She crinkles her nose as she sucks.

"Yeah, you're right. Not too bad once you get past the syrupy goo. I think it's already helping."

She flicks the cough drop around in her mouth, and I force myself to tear my gaze from the way she's working her tongue and licking her lips. "Okay, so no roommate up there?"

"No, why? Wait, do you know Katy?"

"No, I just don't want to scare anyone."

She eyes me, her gaze moving up and down the length of me, which makes me suddenly uncomfortable in the groin area. She taps her chin and concludes, "Yeah, you are kind of scary."

"Hey," I blurt out, feigning offence.

"What?" She sets her glass down and throws her hands up. "I mean, you're huge and if I came out of my bedroom and unexpectedly found you standing in the hall, I'd scream and run. But don't worry. Katy is out with her friends. They do Saturday brunch and then study group."

I don't miss the way she says *her friends* when talking about Katy. If they're roommates, sharing this big house together, are Katy's friends not Jami's friends, too? *Not your business, dude.* I'm about to turn, but stop. "You won't always be so busy, you know. When you finish school maybe you could travel abroad before settling into a job."

"Yeah, maybe. I'm not sure what Theo's plans are."

Fuck. Why does she have to adjust her plan around his? "How about this? How about for the next month, as we see this through, we don't talk about him."

"I guess it only makes sense that if you're my boyfriend, I shouldn't be talking about my ex."

"Yeah, it pisses me off."

She chuckles, probably because she thinks I'm joking, but I'm not. I really don't like the guy, but whatever she sees in him is her business, not mine. I head upstairs and glance into Jami's room. With a desk, dresser, and a bunch of books—I think most are psychology—spread around, it looks like a typical college girl's bedroom. I'm not sure why I expected anything different. Maybe because she doesn't strike me as a typical college girl. There's a deepness about her. Like she's seen more than most.

I walk into the bathroom, grab a towel from the small cabinet and strip off. I dry myself off, and dress in my dry clothes. I shove my damp ones into the bag and step back into the hall. I head back toward the stairs and notice Jami's door is now almost closed. My gaze goes to the crack just in time to see her tug on a dry pair of yoga pants, her sweet ass aimed my way.

I quickly jerk back, and hurry down the stairs, trying to dispel that image from my brain. I do not want to be thinking about her body during our drive home.

I walk to the kitchen, pick up the glass she'd already used and fill it with water. I sip on it and a few minutes later, she appears in the doorway. "Much better," she says and tugs on her T-shirt. "What did you do with your wet things?"

"In my bag."

"I'm going to toss a load into the washer. I'll leave a note asking Katy to switch it. Why don't we toss in your clothes? You can get them when we come back tomorrow."

"Yeah, okay."

I pick up my bag and follow her to the washer and dryer in the hall. I add my wet clothes to hers. What is it about washing our underwear in the same machine that makes this all so intimate?

"Do you think they'll get along in there?" I ask—a bad joke, I know—as she tosses in a soap pod. She gives me a confused look. "I mean, we are on opposing teams. Maybe we'll come back and find our clothes in a tangled mess or shredded to pieces."

She closes the lid. "Well, may the best outfit win." She turns the dial. "I guess we'll find out tomorrow. Are you good to go?"

"Yup." She heads to the kitchen to leave a note for her room-mate, and I pick up my near empty duffle bag, along with Jami's, which doesn't have much in it either.

"You travel light."

"I still have stuff at home too."

Outside, I put our bags in the back and climb into the passenger's seat. She slides into the driver's seat and says, "One more stop. Then we're on our way." I give her a confused look. "The restaurant, remember?"

"Right." I glance down, my mind racing. "Is your brother going to be pissed off?" I wave a finger back and forth between us. "You know...the bet...us. I mean, if you were my sister and someone pulled a stunt like that."

"I guess we'll find out."

I rub my palms on my jeans. "Shit, Jami. I don't want any trouble with your brother. A chef has big knives," I joke half-heartedly.

She laughs. "I'm kidding. Kellan likes everyone and they like him."

"Did he like...." I stop myself before I voice her boyfriend's name. I'm the one who said we weren't going to talk about him. "You know."

She pulls onto the street. "I don't know. I think so."

I cock my head. "He never said?"

"No, actually. They never really spent any time together."

"You and your brother are close though, right?" Did she say that or do I just get the sense?

"Yes, but he's been crazy busy getting his restaurant going, and I've been helping when I can. Th—er, I mean my ex-boyfriend, was always too busy to help out."

I nod. Maybe Kellan doesn't like Theo either, and maybe we'll end up being great friends. I tap my thumb on my leg as she drives and wave to a few people I know as we pass them walking down the street.

"Have your parents met him? Does he go home with you on the weekends?"

"For a guy who doesn't want to talk about my ex, you sure do have a lot of questions." She smirks at me, and I'm about to agree and change the subject when she adds, "No, and no. I mean, they know him, we grew up together, but he hasn't been driving back with me. He's pretty busy. Our fathers probably know each other, both being in the military, but again, it's a big base so who knows."

"What are you studying?" I ask. "I saw the psychology books."

"I'm studying to be a social worker."

"Ah, the volunteering with children. I get it. That sounds like hard work."

"It is."

"What drew you to social work? It's a far cry from a wannabe archery and axe throwing competitor who talked about growing up to be an astronaut."

"I just..." She puckers her lips. "I don't know really. I just think...I guess I want to make a positive difference in a child's life. I want them to know they're important and have value."

Why do I get the feeling this has something to do with her own childhood?

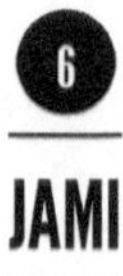

JAMI

fter circling for ten minutes, I finally find a parking spot just off Spring Garden Road. It's always busy on a Saturday, everyone out shopping, and I really hope that's good for Kellan's new business. I parallel park and call up my app to add time to my meter.

"This shouldn't take too long," I tell Kai. He's still looking a bit unsure and I can't understand that. "Don't worry. I'm not going to tell him you won me in a bet. I'm just going to tell him you're a friend from back home."

"Yeah, okay." He nods and steps from the vehicle. I meet him on the sidewalk and we maneuver around the crowd. Delicious scents of rich coffee and freshly baked goods reach my nostrils when Kai pulls open the restaurant door and we're greeted with chatter from those enjoying a late lunch.

"Nice, isn't it?" I ask and take in Kai as he glances around and nods to a few people he knows. I take his hand and drag him to the back.

"Are we allowed back here?"

I laugh. "Of course, my brother owns it." I spot Kellan stir-frying vegetables, and when he sees me, he gestures to his sous chef to take over and comes our way, his arms spread wide. I hug him back. "Full crowd out there," I say, stating the obvious.

"We're running behind," he tells me.

"I won't keep you."

"No, no. Come on. I packed you a lunch for the road." His gaze strays to Kai, and since my brother is only my height, his growth potential stunted thanks to his childhood disease, his head lifts. "Oh, hey."

"Kellan, this is Kai. He's my friend from Scotia Academy. The hockey player I was telling you about."

"Oh."

Kai looks surprised that I was talking about him and I explain, "I told him about your team's fundraiser today and why I was getting so much coffee."

Kellan makes a tsking sound. "Hanging out with the rivals. You're going to get yourself in all kinds of trouble," he points out, but there's humor in his voice.

"Is lunch ready?" I reach for my wallet, and Kellan puts his hand over mine. "You know your money is no good here."

"Is mine?" Kai asks.

"Friend and family discount for you today, which is one hundred percent off." My brother is about to move, then goes perfectly still, his eyes narrowing like they always do when he's 'cooking' something up, something other than food.

"What?" I ask and brace myself. What is he up to?

He folds his arms as someone behind him rings a bell at the serving counter, and yells "order up!"

"I can extend that friend and family discount, Kai. Until the end of the month."

"Oh no," I say, knowing he's scheming up something. "Forget it. We're paying."

"What do you have in mind?"

"People are already calling and booking group parties for Halloween, and Christmas, if you can believe it."

"That's great news, Kellan."

"Sure, but we're brand new and I don't know if we can handle the volume. We're barely keeping up with the lunch crowd. I plan to hire more staff, but we all have to learn to choreograph our movements in this small kitchen."

"Then hire a choreographer," I suggest, having an idea where he's going with this, and not at all sure I like it.

He waves a dismissive hand my way. "That won't work." He continues to stare at Kai.

"What do you have in mind?" Kai asks again.

"Don't entertain him," I warn and Kellan's smile widens, because he's sure he's got Kai, hook, line and sinker.

"How about the first weekend in October, we throw an early Halloween party for your team? You've been on a winning streak lately, haven't you?"

I'm honestly surprised he knows that, but this is a small college town and word spreads fast. Is it possible he heard what happened between Kai and Theo? "Kellan, no. You can't do that."

"Oh, then how about we throw a birthday party for you instead?" I'm pretty sure the color just drained to my toes. While I appreciate my brother wanting to make me the center of attention, how embarrassing would it be to have no one to invite? I could always invite Theo's circle, but I don't think they like me and right now, and Theo and I are broken up.

"I didn't know you had a birthday coming up," Kai says.

"It's no big deal and it's not until December." It's never been a big deal and while there is a small, selfish part of me that always hated that, I am not going to have a party where no one shows up. "I don't like parties."

"Then a Halloween party?" Kellan asks Kai. "For your team."

I lean into him. "Shouldn't you be asking *Theo's* team?" I say Theo under my breath. "You just met Kai and Theo is from Greenwood and it's always been Greenwood against Middleton."

"Kai is here, Theo isn't." Did he just say Theo's name with distaste. Maybe I'm imagining things. He's never said anything bad about Theo before. Actually, he doesn't ever really bring him up. "Besides." He gives me a playful wink. "Brad plays for the Storms."

"Ah, flat white," I say, remembering the special order for Brad. "So that's your sudden interest in hockey."

"Maybe." He wags his brows and turns his attention to the man beside me. "Kai?" he asks again.

"I guess. I'm sure the team would love it, and I mean, I want to help you out. Our city needs a place like this, so it's a win win for everyone." He scrubs that small scar just above his eyebrow. I assume he got that from hockey. "It's up to you, Jami."

While I think it's a horrible idea, I don't want to let my brother down, and Kai is right. His friends would probably love it, and if Kellan is looking for another reason to hang out with Brad, I don't want to be the one to stand in his way.

"There will be food, all free of course, costumes, music. You'd be helping me out big time, Jami."

"I...I guess. If it means this much to you."

He claps just as a plate breaks behind us. "Let me get your food."

We stand there as he disappears for a moment, and Kai dips his head. "Do you really hate birthday parties?"

"Yes."

"I don't know anyone who hates birthday parties."

"Now you do."

He laughs. "I guess I don't much like the parties at Storm House."

"Never been to one."

"You must have been to a few hockey parties at the frat on your campus."

I crinkle my nose. "No, never."

"Not even with...you know."

"He said it was for the players and cheerleaders."

Kai runs agitated fingers through his hair. "Are you fucking..." He stops, shakes his head and takes a deep breath. He glances away and falls silent. A moment of awkwardness surrounds us. He breaks it and asks quietly, "Are you going to come to your brother's Halloween party?"

"I feel like I have to." I suck in air, a bad taste in my mouth. "Do you think I have to dress up?"

"Of course, you do. I'm going as a hockey player," he tells me with a smirk.

"Not fair." I whack him and catching me by surprise, he slides his big fingers around my wrist, and holds my hand to his chest. His strong heart pumps beneath my fingers, and as he tugs me close, his warm heat reaches out to me.

"Since when has life ever been fair?" he asks, far too seriously. My heart leaps.

"Never," I respond.

"Right." He lets my hand go and looks over my head. "I like your brother."

I smile. "I knew you would. I wonder how Brad feels about him."

Kai laughs. "Don't know, and I'm minding my own business. I know nothing about relationships and I am not a matchmaker."

I nod, understanding that. "Kellan could use a good guy in his life." Kai opens his mouth, but shuts it again. Once again I can't help but think I don't want to hear what he has to say. "Is Brad a good guy?"

"He is. Like I said, I know nothing about relationships, but I think I could see them as a couple."

"Why do you say that?"

"Kellan is a chef, and Brad likes food."

That makes me laugh. "Something funny?" Kellan asks with a grin on his face as he presses the large brown paper bag into my hand. His gaze goes back and forth between the two of us, and there's a hint of amusement there, like he knows something we don't. Before I can ask, he says, "Enjoy and thanks again, Kai. I'll text Jami the details once I have them all figured out. Oh, Jami, please text me Kai's number."

"Why do you—"

"Gotta run." He hurries back to the stove, leaving my question unanswered. I turn my focus and weigh the heavy bag in my hands. "Does he think we're starving?"

Kai takes it from me. "If he does, he'd be right. Let's go eat."

I follow him to the door, and try not to stare at his wide shoulders as he walks. A noise sounds at one of the tables and I find a group of girls I don't know leaning toward one another and whispering. I suddenly feel very self-conscious. They're probably wondering why a guy like Kai would be with someone like me. He pushes the door open to let me exit first.

"Did you know those girls in there?" I ask.

"What girls?"

"Oh, just some girls chatting and looking at you." I snort. "They were probably wondering who I was."

He shrugs. "I didn't see them."

I suddenly feel very out of my element with him. "I'm not keeping you from anything, am I?"

"No. My only commitment was the car wash today. Oh, and to help chaperone a dance tonight."

I laugh at that. "If those girls knew I was from Kingston, I'm sure they wouldn't like us together."

"It's not their business."

"Maybe they were whispering because they heard you won me in a bet."

"Again, not any of their business." He stops at the car. "No one is going to say anything to you, Jami. Not when you're with me."

I love his protective instincts. "I can take care of myself."

"I know you can."

I'm not sure how he knows that, and I don't ask. Instead, I circle the car and climb in. He slides into the passenger seat, the bag on his lap. He opens it and peeks. "Damn, this looks good."

"What did he pack?"

"Soup, sandwiches, and a couple of water bottles." He eyes me. "How are you supposed to eat and drive? I could always feed you, I guess."

I laugh. "You are not feeding me."

"Has no one ever fed you before?"

"Sure, when I was an infant."

"What about the nacho?"

"It was just a nacho." I cast him a fast glance. "Do people, and when I say people, I mean girls, feed you often?"

He laughs. "Maybe."

"That's disgusting." Actually, it's not. I kind of liked it when he fed me.

"Don't knock it until you try it, Nichols."

"I am knocking it and you are not feeding me while I drive."

"Fine, we'll wait and starve."

"You can eat, and then if you want, you can take over driving and I can eat."

He gives a fast shake of his head. "No."

I glance at him. He has a jeep, and actually put it up in the bet, so why the harsh reaction? "You don't like driving?" As soon as the question leaves my mouth, I realize what's going on. He lost his friend in a car accident. Maybe he doesn't even drive anymore. "Actually, why don't we stop at that little rest area off the highway, near exit four. You know that one right."

His brow lifts. "You mean the one where that family got robbed last year?"

"Yeah, that's the one. But I'm with you, so I'm not too worried."

"Aww." He rubs his knuckles over my head. "Look at you. You want my protection after all."

Okay, maybe he's got me there. "I might as well take advantage of having you with me." His brow raises. "You're big and scary, remember?"

Grinning, he leans toward me, his warm scent overtaking the delicious smells inside the bag and overwhelming me. "Maybe it's me you need to worry about." He gives an exaggerated gasp and sits back, pushing against the door. "Wait, maybe I should be worried about you." His eyes are big, his demeanor playful as he glances at the bag and then back at me. "Are you luring me into the woods with delicious food so you can take *advantage* of me?"

That makes me laugh, hard. "Are you that easy, Kai?"

"Yeah, I might be," he says, a sheepish look on his face that tugs at something inside me. I just shake my head and concentrate on the busy city streets as he places the bag at his feet. "For the record, I do consider you my responsibility." Now it's my turn to raise my brow. "I won you in a bet. That means you're mine to take care of."

"I think you're thinking of the Chinese proverb, if you save a life that life is your responsibility."

"Yup," is all he mutters and it makes me wonder if he thinks he's saving me from something, or someone. I continue to drive, and once I hit the highway, I glance at him, noticing how quiet he's become, not to mention the way he stares at the highway with laser sharp focus, especially when a vehicle speeds past us. What is going through his mind?

"Getting hungry?" I ask.

"Starved." He glances at me. "Your brother wasn't at all what I expected."

Is that what he's been thinking about? "What did you expect?"

"I guess I don't really know. You two are the same height. For some reason, I expected him to be taller. Maybe because he's older. You could pass as twins." He's joking, but he doesn't know the truth behind Kellan's height.

"Kellan was very sick when he was young. Childhood leukemia," I say, my words shocking myself. I don't usually talk about my brother. His business is his, and if he wants someone to know he was sick, that's up to him to share.

"I'm sorry, Jami." There's such warmth and sincerity in his voice it pulls me into a place I'm not familiar with—a place of comfort and trust. My heart tightens in my chest as I steal a fast glance at the man barely able to fit into my passenger seat. Do I trust Kai? I don't know but I think we both have deep rooted fears. "I didn't know," he adds quietly, his fingers landing gently on my wrist. "I guess that's why he was never in any sports?"

"Yeah," I agree and then I have no idea why, or what's driving me, but I blurt out, "The only reason I was born was to save him."

7

KAI

"Jesus, Jami."

I tighten my hands on her arm, my fingers pressing into her soft flesh as she blinks rapidly, like she didn't mean to say what she just said.

"I'm sorry." Her curls bounce around her shoulder as she shakes her head. She snorts like it's nothing, like she wants to brush it off. "I don't know why I just said that. I shouldn't have."

"No, it's okay." Something compelled her to tell me that and I'm pretty sure it wasn't easy so I don't want to brush it off.

"I don't usually talk about that, and I don't want you to think I'm looking for sympathy or anything."

"I don't think that," I tell her as she stares straight ahead. Sure, she's driving but I get the sense she's too embarrassed to look at me. "I like how close you two are."

She smiles and nods. She clearly loves him a lot, and now, a lot of things make sense, like why she was sheltered. Her parents were terrified of losing their children and that's legit, but I hate that she feels like she was only born to save her sibling. I'm sure it's not true, but that doesn't mean it doesn't feel that way to her. "What did you guys like to do when you were little?"

"We loved board games and puzzles and video games."

"I never took you for a video game girl."

"Honestly, I don't love them. But Kellan did."

"And you wanted to make him happy."

"Always."

"What did he do to make you happy?" I ask and the question seems to take her by surprise.

"I..." She hesitates and cocks her head. "I guess I never really thought about it." She grins. "I guess there was one thing."

I like her smile, it brightens up the entire car. "Tell me."

"Promise not to tell."

I laugh. "You and your secrets, but okay, I promise." I like having secrets with her, which is odd, because secrets bring people together and I don't want to get close to her. That is not my goal here.

Why then did you agree to go home with her this weekend?

"We lived on the military base. Still do. Well, my parents still do. There was a big tree in our backyard." She glances at me, her head dipped, her eyes half lidded and full of mischief. "We weren't supposed to climb it."

"But of course, you climbed it, Jami," I snort, admiring her adventurous spirit. I used to have that spirit myself. It's been gone for four long years. "You probably shouldn't have been climbing it, though."

She throws one arm out and makes a huffing sound. "How else was I going to see the ballfield and the games going on if I didn't climb it?"

"A ballfield you weren't allowed to play on?"

"Uh huh. I don't really think Kellan was much into climbing." She stares straight ahead, like her thoughts are a million miles away, and I wait. "But he always did it with me."

"When your parents weren't looking."

"Which wasn't often," she tells me. "But there were times when Dad was at work—he's a pilot—and Mom had to run to the store. She stayed home with us."

"My guess is Kellan was looking out for you, the same way you were always looking out for him." I love their relationship and could feel the care they had for one another at the restaurant.

She turns to me, her smile widening. "I never thought about it like that before." Her hand slides across the seat and she gives mine a little squeeze. "Thanks." A beat of silence and then, "Do you have siblings?" My heart stops beating for a good ten seconds. "Kai?"

Cooper wasn't my brother by birth, but he was definitely my brother and he's not here today because of me. Isn't that interesting. If I wasn't born, Cooper would be alive, and if Jami wasn't born, her brother might not have survived his childhood disease. What a fucking mess we are.

"No, just me. My parents own the big vineyard just outside of Middleton," I say, rambling on just so the pain of Cooper's loss doesn't rise up and punch me in the throat. "It's actually harvest time. I'll probably help them pick tomorrow. They don't need the help, they have staff, but I like being in the vineyard."

"Ward Winery?" she says excitedly. "Your parents own A-Ward Winning Winery?"

"You know it?"

"I've heard of it, of course. Their wine has won tons of awards. I can't believe I didn't put that together." She gives a small chuckle. "The vineyard expanded over the years. They even do weddings there now."

I grin. "I know."

She laughs. "Of course, you know. Why wouldn't you know?" Her eyes light up. "Maybe there's one going on this weekend."

"Yeah, I never thought to check. I just thought I'd surprise my folks. Why? Do you want to see a wedding?"

She shrugs. "I don't know. Not really, I guess. Have you seen many?"

"Plenty, I usually help staff them."

"That sounds like fun."

"It's not," I tell her and she grins as she flicks on her signal light and pulls off at the rest spot. She parks and I climb out of the car. There's one other car there, a family including a mother, father and a boy around seven are sitting at a picnic table. They eye us carefully but I wave and plunk our food down at the table far away from them.

"I'm starving," Jami says as I open the bag and take out two containers with soup. I slide one to her and reach in and pull out our sandwiches.

"Oh, there's a couple of apples here I didn't see."

She laughs. "My brother and his apple a day keeps the doctor away theory." She opens the lid to her soup and breathes it in as I hand her a spoon.

"You don't like apples?"

"When we were little, we owned a tree at Dempsey corner," she tells me. "They had this 'support a tree' program. We used to pick apples every fall."

"Were you allowed to climb that tree?" I ask.

She laughs. "Of course not. We used a ladder, or my father would lift me." She sighs. "I loved that place and their three-legged dog."

I nod as old happy memories grip me. "Yeah, I remember him."

"He was the sweetest and the laziest."

"What was his name again?" I ask.

"Frankfurt," she says absently, like she too is thinking of happy times. "Did you pick apples there?"

"Yeah, well sort of. We didn't own a tree or anything. Coop and I..." I begin and my words fall off as my stomach tightens. "I uh...I'm just saying my best friend and I used to sneak onto the orchard and gorge on apples. I was probably eating from your tree."

Her mouth gapes open. "No way."

"Hell, I don't know," I say. "Could have been, though."

"Fine." She takes a spoonful of soup and swallows. "You owe me a bag of apples."

I snort. "I owe you more than a bag. We ate like six at a time. Good thing Frankfurt was the laziest. He didn't even chase us off, he just sat with us."

"I would have bitten you."

"You bite, Jami?" I joke.

She looks a bit flustered as she shakes her head. "No, I meant if I was Frankfurt. He should have bitten you for eating my apples. You owe me." She glances at my arms as I unwrap my sandwich. "My brother was right, an apple a day and all does pay off. Or in your case, six a day."

I angle my head and take in the way her gaze is raking over my body. I probably shouldn't like the way she's admiring me. "Was that a compliment, Nichols?"

"No, what I meant to say is maybe that's why you're so big and scary. All those apples."

"Right," I laugh and pull the lid off my soup. Delicious scents fill my nostrils and I breathe it in as I dip my spoon into the deep yellow broth. I note the way Jami is still watching me as I slide the spoon into my mouth and moan. "This is delicious."

"Right?" she says. "Kellan will be happy to hear you approve. I bet he's going to do a delicious spread for the party."

I bite into my sandwich, enjoying the chicken and crunch of apple and walnuts. "I'm not sure I'll ever be able to eat a peanut butter sandwich again." I chew and swallow. I wink at her. "That's not entirely true. It's kind of my go to when I'm too lazy to cook."

She winks back. "Stick with me, friend, and Kellan will always extend the friend and family discount."

I frown, because it reminds me that I don't have friends, nor do I want them. Nothing good can come from that. We might be pretending to be a couple or something, because of a stupid bet with douche bag extraordinaire, but when it comes right down to it, she's not even my friend.

I hear voices and my gaze strays to the boy at the far end of the open rest area as he kicks a soccer ball around, calling on his dad to join him. It's a shame Jami and her brother missed out on playing sports. I have a feeling Jami would have excelled at anything she put her mind to. I take another bite of my sandwich, and turn back to find Jami staring at me. Yeah, okay, I did drift off there for a second?

"Tell me what it's like chaperoning a military family resource dance," I say.

She bites into her sandwich, chews and then begins to animatedly tell me about all the drama at the dances. "Who would have thought there'd be so much drama between girls at the pre-teen age?"

"You must have known. Weren't you a pre-teen girl once?" I joke. "Or am I missing something?"

"I didn't really...I mean, I didn't go to the dances." She crinkles up her nose. "I never liked to leave my brother at home. He didn't have a lot of friends, you know. Being home and being sick a lot. I think he's making up for it now. Wanting to get in with your hockey team." She shrugs. "I wouldn't have enjoyed it anyway. I don't know how to dance."

"No one knows how to dance. You just flail your arms and legs around, Nichols," I joke, as I do exactly that, which makes her laugh, and while I like the sound, I understand there's more to her not going to dances than just not being able to dance. Her parents probably never let her go, and I wonder if she even had friends growing up. "You like it?" I ask. She angles her head. "Chaperoning these dances?" I clarify.

"I like the kids. I enjoy being with them, and most times I'm able to help with the drama." She grabs a napkin and wipes her mouth and I try not to stare at those kissable lips. "It usually stems from jealousy and I help them work it out."

"You're going to be a great social worker."

Her smile is full of gratitude. "Thanks."

"No one is going to be upset that I'm going to be there?" I finish my sandwich and crinkle up the wrapper, tossing it back into the paper bag. "You know, the enemy from Middleton."

She exhales and her shoulders sag. "At our age, aren't we all past that?"

"You'd think," I snort out as my mind goes back to her asshole ex-boyfriend, who will be her boyfriend again once this charade is over. Not that I should care, but dammit, I do.

Just then her phone pings and she pulls it from her pocket. I don't need to ask to know it's douche bag.

"He's not supposed to be texting," I point out.

"I know."

I hold my hand out. "Can I?"

She hands the phone over and I message Theo, letting him know it's me and that he's breaking the rules, and he knows what that means. I grin when he texts back, telling me to go fuck myself. I hand the phone back and as Jami reads over our exchange, I hear a yelp. I turn to see the soccer ball barreling our way and I jump up and stop it with my foot. I bounce it around on the top of my foot and then kick it back to the boy. He thanks me and I don't bother sitting back down. Instead, I clean up as Jami stares at me.

"I didn't know you played soccer too."

"Yup, I like all sports. Played them all. But now I have my sights set on the NHL."

"Played them all, huh?" she teases. "Even curling."

I put one hand on my hip and eye her. "Is that really a sport?" I joke.

She groans and shakes her head, her blue eyes losing a bit of their shine. "Not you too," she grumbles.

My smile falls. "What?"

"You know who...well, he felt the same way. Curling wasn't a sport."

"Hey," I say when her head drops. She lifts it and my gaze latches onto hers. "I'm only messing with you. I know it's a sport. When is your next game? I'll put it in my calendar." I'm pretty sure her eyes just bugged out of her head, which leads me to believe douche bag never supported her. "Wait, is it called a game?" I'm being very sincere even though she's looking at me with skeptical eyes. "Or is it called a match?"

"It's a game, and we have ends, which are like innings," she explains.

"Ah, like baseball. I guess I'd better brush up on my curling lingo."

"I'm sure you're not serious, Kai."

"You'll see." She crinkles up her sandwich wrapper and I check the time and gesture toward the car. "Should we get out of here? We don't want to be driving in the dark."

She looks at me like I was an alien speaking a foreign language. "It's not even dinner time yet."

"The nights are getting dark earlier," I explain. What I don't explain is that I no longer like to be on the highway at night. Jaunting around town I can do, but the highway, forget about it.

We clean up, drop our garbage into the trash can and walk to the car. I slide in as the little boy yelps and runs after his ball again. It comes our way so I kick it back. When I get into the car, Jami glances at me.

"If you played all sports, why did you decide to concentrate on hockey?"

8

KAI

I realize she told me something difficult and private, and maybe I owe her the same. I can't push the words through my lips though, can't bring myself to talk about Cooper with anyone. It still hurts so fucking much and like everyone else, she'll probably think horrible things about me, or wonder why a great guy like Coop died instead of me. I tense as she starts the car and struggle for something to say.

"I guess I was just better at hockey," I fib, and try to sound normal when my insides are a torn, tangled mess.

"I've seen you play." She nudges me playfully. "You're all right."

I chuckle at that, and push back in my seat as she waits for an opening in traffic and pulls back onto the highway. Changing the subject, I ask, "Are you planning to stay in Nova Scotia after you get your degree?"

She nods. "I want to work with military families."

"Your choices are Greenwood, Halifax or Shearwater?"

"Lots of options. But I do like being in the city."

"Me too."

"Do you want to play for a Canadian team or do you want to go to the States?"

"I'd love to play for Edmonton. I know a few guys on the team and the Boston Bucks are really doing well too. There are a few former Storm players there, too."

"You don't want to go somewhere warm like Miami?" She looks me over. "I guess that's a stupid question."

"Why?"

"You run hot. You only wear a shirt or sweater, even on cold nights."

"Yeah. I like the cold weather better." I don't tell her the truth, that I don't feel like I deserve any kind of comfort. A song comes on the radio that she likes and she sings along as we drive. She actually has a nice voice. We talk about school and sports and she tells me more about her curling. I listen with interest, which seems to surprise her.

"Do you mind if I ask how you got hooked up with...him?" She's a beautiful woman, any guy would want her, but those two they don't seem compatible.

Hurt briefly flashes in her eyes as she glances my way. "I know. I'm not your typical puck bunny or cheerleader." She swallows and the sound guts me.

I put my hand on her arm. "I'm not saying that, Jami. You're gorgeous." I pause, but she doesn't respond to the compliment and I think it's because she might not believe it. "I'm just saying, you're driven and selfless and want to make a difference in this world. Your ex cares only about himself."

"That's what he says about you," she answers quietly.

"Do you believe that?"

A moment of silence and then, "No." She stares straight ahead in thought, and while she doesn't owe me an answer, I didn't tell her the real reason behind wanting a hockey career, she opens up and explains, "Things sort of happened after I used the campus security app."

I nod. A lot of the guys at Storm House volunteer for our security app too, keeping students safe by walking them home after parties and things like that. I haven't done a stint. I volunteer at the hospital and charity auctions.

"I was taking a course over the summer. It was getting dark and I just had a weird feeling someone was following me, so I used the app and he showed up right away to walk me."

"Showed up right away? Maybe he was the one stalking you?"

She looks at me like I'm insane. "Why would he ever stalk me?"

"I don't know. I can't say why he does the things he does." But I do have a strange feeling, though, about their whole relationship.

She brushes that off. "I was actually kind of surprised that he asked for my number and texted me the next day. I mean, we knew each other from Greenwood but never hung out in the same crowd."

"You shouldn't be surprised."

"I am surprised. Guys like him don't bother with girls like me."

"You were flattered." She curls her shoulders like she's embarrassed by that. "Nothing wrong with being flattered, Jami," I tell her. I just wish it was by a different guy.

As if on autopilot, she flicks on her signal and takes the exit to Greenwood. "Are you taking me to your place?" I ask, because my exit is the next one.

Her eyes go wide. "Oh shoot, sorry. I just thought you'd be coming to my place. You must want to go home first, and see your parents."

I shrug. "No, it's okay. They don't even know I'm home anyway. I can go home after the dance." Although it will be after dark and that makes me extremely uncomfortable. I shift in my seat and glance out the side window to hide my unease.

Traffic is thick along the secondary road and she slows. "So, you're sure I'm not going to get mobbed or anything?" I tease. "Stepping into the enemy's territory?" I jokingly glance around. "You don't have a trap set, do you?"

"No, and don't worry. I'll protect you."

I laugh at that as we drive around her old stomping grounds. She goes through town and heads toward base housing. She points to the family resource center as we pass. "That's where the dance is held. We can walk there, my house is just over here." She takes a corner and pulls into a driveway and I take in the house, which is exactly like every other house on the street.

"How can you tell which one is yours?" I joke.

"Mom hangs a wreath every season." I take in the wreath with the orange leaves around it. "It's the way I can find my way home."

"Right," I say with a laugh and open the car door. I climb out and stretch out my arms as she pops the trunk to get her bag.

"Do you need yours?"

I shake my head. "No, leave it for later."

I take her bag from her and shoulder it as we walk to her front door and I don't miss the way a few women who are walking their small dogs along the sidewalk slow to watch us. I gesture with a nod as they blatantly stare.

"Does gossip spread here as fast as it does on campus?"

"You can't sneeze without it being reported," she tells me and politely waves to the women watching us, even though there's revulsion on her face. "Dog walkers' club," she explains. "They know everything about everyone and when they can't get dirt, they make it up."

She turns back to me, and my gaze drops to her lush lips as she puckers them in distaste. "I take it you don't much like them?"

She puts her hand on the doorknob. "Nope."

I grin and close my hand over hers before she can open the door. "Should we give them something to talk about, then?"

She raises her brow. "What do you have in mind?"

Before I can think better of it, and maybe I don't want to, because fuck, I've been dying to press my lips to hers since that fast kiss at the car wash, I put my hand around her head, and give a little tug on her hair. Her head tilts upward and her lips part and a groan I have zero control over crawls out of my throat as I dip my head and close my lips over hers. Fuck...I'm not sure what I expected, maybe for her to knee me in the nuts, but she doesn't. Nope, she doesn't do that at all. Instead, she wraps her arms around my waist and actually steps into me. I deepen the kiss, our tongues tangling, and we stay like that until one of the yappy dogs bark.

I press my forehead to hers, not wanting her to move, otherwise she'll see my boner. "Wrong," is all I mutter.

Her eyes widen, worry dancing in them. "What…yeah, no you're right. This was wr—"

"Jami," I whisper and her she stops talking. "You were wrong when you said you weren't made of sugar, because babe, you sure taste sweet."

She takes a fast breath, and slides her tongue over her bottom lip. "You do too," she tells me.

"You think I'm sweet?" She nods. "Now that's a secret of mine you'll have to carry around."

She shakes her head like she's coming out of a stupor, and nods. "Right, okay."

"I'm kidding, Jami."

Just then the door opens and I step back as a woman who is obviously Jami's mother stands there, her gaze going back and forth between the two of us. "I thought I heard noise out here."

I hope the noise she heard wasn't me moaning after kissing her daughter.

"Hey Claire," one of the dog walking ladies says and Claire waves back.

"Hey Donna, nice day for a walk." It's easy to tell Claire likes them about as much as Jami. She turns her attention back to her daughter. "I didn't know you were bringing company."

"Mom, this is Kai Ward. Kai, this is my mom, Claire. Kai lives in Middleton and is actually helping me with the dance tonight. I'm going to drive him home later."

Her big blue eyes narrow in on me as I set Jami's bag on the floor. "Oh, are you a student at Kingston too?"

"No, actually," I begin. "I go to Scotia Academy." I grin at her. "We're rival schools." Her mother's eyes narrow even more and I can't blame her, so I explain. "Jami helped us with a carwash today to raise money for the children's hospital, so I thought I'd help her at the dance tonight." I naturally keep out the truth that we're together because of a bet.

She nods like that all makes sense, which it really doesn't. "That is lovely. Jami loves to help out the kids. Anything she can do, she will." She stands back. "Come on in. Are you hungry? How was the drive?"

"Drive was good. Kellan packed us a big picnic. I probably won't eat for a week."

"How is Kellan?" she asks, the fine lines around her eyes crinkling with worry.

"He's great, Mom. His restaurant is amazing. It was packed when we stopped in."

"I don't like him working so hard."

"He seems to love what he's doing. He's actually going to hold a big Halloween party for the Storms hockey team."

"You play hockey?" Claire asks me. I nod and confusion once again fills her eyes. "You play against Theo's college? I know how competitive those two teams are."

"It's all good, Mom," Jami assures her, but I think she's smart enough to sense something about this whole situation is off, and it worries her.

"What smells so good?" I ask, changing the subject.

"I just made cinnamon rolls," Claire tells us, her voice a bit quieter. It's easy to tell how much she cares for and worries about her kids and I really want to tell her that nothing bad will ever happen to Jami when she's with me.

"I am too full," Jami groans.

"Hey, there's always room for cinnamon rolls," I pipe in and Claire seems to like that.

"When is Dad home?" Jami asks. "We have to leave here in an hour to go to the resource center."

We follow Claire to the kitchen. "Not until later tonight. He'll be happy to see you."

The phone rings, and Claire goes to get it. She talks quietly, and I can't help but wonder if it's one of the dog walkers filling her in on our escapades on the doorstep. Maybe I shouldn't have done that.

Jami pulls one of the gooey cinnamon rolls from the pan and puts it on a plate. "Mom makes the best cinnamon rolls," she tells me, and hands me the plate. I tug off a piece and put it in my mouth. "Delicious." I tug another piece off and hold it out for her and she opens her mouth to me.

She bites into it and moans. "You do realize you just let me feed you, you know?"

She chuckles. "Yeah, I guess."

I walk to the patio door leading to a deck and she follows me. I glance at her backyard and take in the trees and shrubbery and the big fence that was erected to keep Jami and Kellan safe. It must have been hard for Jami to stifle her spirit and it guts me to think she believes she was only born to save her brother. It was easy to tell how much her mother cared about her, but we all see and feel things differently and those are issues she's going to have to work through.

That almost brings a laugh to my throat, because yeah, I get it. I have a shit ton of issues to work through too, but I don't think anything or anyone can ever help me feel whole again.

Claire hangs up the phone and reaches for her purse. "I have to run out. The fabric I was waiting on just arrived."

"Mom likes to quilt," Jami explains.

"I'll see you tonight, Jami, and it was great meeting you, Kai."

She disappears out the front door, and Jami opens the patio door and steps out. She leans over the railing, pointing her sweet ass my way. Fuck. My dick instantly thickens and I give myself a hard lecture to get my shit under control. I am not getting involved with Jami, and that kiss, while amazing, was a fucking mistake.

Even though I know it, I find myself saying, "We have the whole place to ourselves and an hour before we volunteer." I glance around the private backyard. "What do you think we should do?"

Jesus, Kai, what the fuck is wrong with you?

She glances at me over her shoulder, and I note the twinkle in her eyes. "I have an idea."

"Oh yeah, what are you thinking?"

"Well, it involves wood and climbing."

Jesus Christ if she's talking about climbing over my wood, I'm not sure I have the strength to say no.

Walk away dude, just walk the fuck away.

"Tell me more," I plead, stepping into her.

JAMI

"Did you have fun?" I ask Kai as we walk down the road toward the resource center, my hip bumping his as I sway back and forth on the edge of the curb.

"Yeah, it was okay," he says and scrubs his face as he stares off into the distance. For a moment back there on the deck, when I mentioned climbing and wood, he shifted, looking somewhat uncomfortable. Did he think I meant something else? If he did, and I can only imagine what he was thinking—he's a young, healthy virile male after all. But what I really wonder is, was he shifting uneasily because he liked or disliked the idea?

"Didn't I tell you?" I spread my arms wide. "You can see the whole ball field from the top of the tree."

"You did," he says a hint of worry in his voice. "I think you went up too high, though. You could have hurt yourself."

I grin at him. "Sorry, Mom."

He laughs and throws his arm around me. "I just don't want you to fall and crack your skull open or anything."

I snuggle into the warmth of his body, even though I'm the one with a coat on and he's only in a T-shirt. "Worried about me, Ward?"

"I told you, for the next month, you're my responsibility whether I like it or not. I made the stupid bet, so I have to live by the consequences."

My insides crumble a bit, although I really don't have a right to be that upset. He might have wanted to bet on me to piss off Theo, but it was my boyfriend who agreed. Whether Kai likes me or not, or dislikes that he's responsible for me now, shouldn't matter one bit to me.

Then why does it?

I stare at the ground, my body stiff as we walk. "Wait, I didn't mean it like that, Jami," he says, clearly picking up on my sudden quietness. "You're not a consolation prize or anything. I mean, you agree the bet was stupid and I shouldn't have involved you. I only did it to piss *him* off."

I kick a pebble and it clacks against the ground. "I know it had nothing to do with me."

He frowns and opens his mouth, but closes it again, and I'm glad. I don't really need him to verify what I already know.

Up ahead, numerous cars turn down the road to the resource center. "Looks like a packed house," I say, changing the subject.

"So, what is my role?" He flexes his biceps. "Bouncer?"

I grin at him, even though my stomach flutters as I take in his powerful body. "They're kids. You will not be muscling them around."

Muscling me around however....

Good God, get it together, girl.

We walk by the outdoor pool, which is shut down for the evening. "Did you swim there as a child?"

"I took lessons for a while." I nudge him. "Maybe we can sneak in later."

"Wow, I'm going to get myself in trouble if I hang out with you." He glances at me. "What actually is there to do here in Greenwood?"

"Probably a lot more than there is to do in Middleton."

"Oh, we're going there are we," he says and pulls me to him. "A fight on which small town is better?"

"No need to fight. I win hands down." I start listing off all the activities offered through the base and he nods as he listens.

"But did you ever lay down in a vineyard at night, and just smell the grapes and look at the constellations in the sky?"

"No, never. How boring," I respond, but I'm joking. It sounds just about perfect.

"Right, I forgot, you're a daredevil."

"Jami," Samantha calls out when she sees me and gives me a big wave. I wave back.

"Hey, Sam."

"Do you know all their names?"

"I'm here pretty much every week. We'll have to keep our eye on Sam tonight. She and Olivia are both after Ryan, and Ryan is playing them. I don't want anyone's feelings hurt."

"Should I have a talk with Ryan?"

I grin at him. "Why are you going to give him pointers on how to be a better *player?*"

"Hey," he says and gives me a little shove. "That's not fair." He crinkles his nose. "Well, I mean, it might have been fair, but now I've got a *girlfriend,*" he says jokingly.

"You're a one girl kind of man, Ward?"

"I guess I would be. I've never been down that road before, so this is all kind of new to me."

"And fake," I remind him.

Except for that kiss. That didn't feel fake at all. It felt...so nice.

"Okay, let's do this," he says and pulls open the glass door when we reach it. I enter and he holds it open to a group of girls who just climbed out of a SUV. I turn back and wave to the mom driving.

The girls all giggle and whisper when they get past Kai, and Laura turns to me and asks, "Who's that?"

"That's Kai and he's helping out tonight."

"Is he your boyfriend?" she asks. "If he's not, I get dibs," she says to her friends, and I shake my head. Laura is twelve going on twenty and her parents are in for some tough years.

I lift my head and find Kai grinning at me, having overheard the conversation. He steps up to me and puts his arm around my shoulder to end speculation and more giggles ensue.

Laura grabs Cassie's arm. "Come on, let's go see who's here." They take off into the room where the lights are just a bit dimmed for the dance.

There's a small office just outside the big community room where the dance is held. I step inside and find Jim, a full-time manager at the resource center, putting his files away. He's usually in a T-shirt and jeans, but tonight he's in a nice button down, with khaki pants, and I'm pretty sure I smell cologne. "Hey, Jami," he says and hands over the keys for me to lock up tonight. There's a key drop outside the door where I'll put the keys back in.

"Everything ready? DJ's here?"

"He's setting up and you're good to go." He hurries out from around the desk. "Thanks again for always being so reliable."

"You look like you're in a hurry."

He grins. "I have a date."

That makes me happy. He's a sweet guy and deserves to find someone nice, especially after his wife's affair last year. But that's not easy for a middle-aged man in a small town. What sucked for him was that the details of the affair went through the whole community. Apparently, his ex-wife hooked up with a pilot and now they're both stationed out in Comox. I'm glad he doesn't have to face her every day. That would be brutal.

"Have a great time." He smiles when he sees Kai behind me. "My friend Kai will be helping out tonight," I tell him and he eyes me curiously, because yes, he knows I have a boyfriend named Theo.

"Okay, you two have fun."

He hurries out the door and I turn to Kai. "This is where you can come if it all gets too much for you," I tell Kai as I take a book from the drawer and write in our names.

Just then the smell of perfume overwhelms my senses and without looking up, I say, "Gwen is here."

"What the hell?" Kai waves his hand in front of his face.

"Is she in her thigh high black heels?"

He turns and groans. "Jesus."

"I know," I agree. "She's a sweet kid, and I think she sneaks those boots out when her mother isn't looking." I glance around his body and wave to Gwen. "I'd get a nosebleed that high up," I joke. "Do you want to help out with the treats table?"

"Sure. You know I like sweets."

Okay, what does he mean by that? Is he referencing our kiss? Which shouldn't have happened and can't happen again. I walk around the desk, and he doesn't move, which forces me to brush past his body, and I swear to God, a moan just rose in his throat.

He follows me into the auditorium and I guide him to the table. "Here is the price list, and the candy bars and chips are in the boxes. The cooler has water and soda."

"Sounds easy enough." He grabs a box and sets it on the table and our hands connect as we both make a move to open it. Okay, there is no way electricity should be zinging through my body right now.

"Sorry." I pull my hand back and let him open it.

"How do you manage to do this all yourself?"

I shrug. "I don't always have to. There are other volunteers. High school students looking for volunteer credits." I glance up to see Mila coming into the room. "As a matter of fact, here comes one now."

"Mila." I wave her over. Her gaze goes from me to Kai, and her eyes widen a bit.

"Hey, Jami," she calls out, without ever taking her eyes off Kai. Okay, I realize he's nice to look at, but straight up ogling is rude and he's too old for her anyway.

"Mila, this is Kai. He's helping out tonight. So, if you have plans you don't have to stay. I'll still give you the credit."

She steps up to Kai. "Hi Kai," she practically murmurs as she flicks her long hair back. She casts me a fast glance over her shoulder, then turns back to Kai. "I have no plans. Brad and I broke up, so I'm free tonight," she says and the weirdest burst of jealousy goes through me.

"I'm sorry to hear about your breakup," I tell her.

"He was just so...juvenile. I need a real man in my life."

Oh, good God.

"Do you go to Kingston with Jami?" she asks Kai.

"I actually go to Scotia Academy."

"Oh, rival schools. What are you doing here then?"

Before I can hear his answer, I hear my name called, and turn to see Sam running out of the room in tears. I catch Kai's glance. "I'd better go take care of that."

He nods, his attention back on Mila as she puts her hand on his arm, wanting his attention back on her. I think what might bother me the most is that she doesn't, for one little second, think I might be with Kai. Like he's out of my league and I'm not a threat to her. I get that she's popular, and the guys fall at her feet, but am I that unimportant to her?

Maybe I am and maybe I'm that unimportant to Theo too. He did, after all, hand me over in a bet.

I head toward the main lobby, and find Sam talking with her friend Brody, her face red as she tries not to cry. A part of me is glad I missed out on all this teen drama, although I'm embroiled deep into the drama between Kai and Theo, and the bet.

"Hey Sam, what's going on?" I ask, even though I know.

She sniffs. "Why does Olivia have to like every guy I like?"

"I'm sorry. Do you want to come into the office for a little break? I can grab you some snacks."

"Okay," she agrees, and Brody starts walking with her.

"I'll come too," he says. It's funny really, she and Brody are so cute together. But she wants what she can't have. Isn't that typical, though, at any age in life. What is it about people? Why do they covet what they can't have?

We head inside the office and Brody sits close to Sam, a look of adoration on his face. "I can get the snacks, Sam. Ketchup chips?" he asks, knowing exactly what she likes and she nods in response. How freaking adorable is Brody? Every girl needs a guy who pays attention to her likes and dislikes the way he does.

"Tell Kai to put the snacks on my tab, okay, Brody?"

"I don't mind buying Sam's snacks."

"Okay, if that's what you want," I concede, because it's clearly what he wants. He hurries from the room and I hand Sam a tissue.

"Sam, you don't want to hear this right now, but boys will come and go. If you want my advice, I'd say find the guy who's going to treat you like you're the most important person in the world to them. You deserve that."

The words rake over my tongue and leave a bitter taste. Honest to God, who am I to give that kind of advice when I'm not taking it myself?

"Laura said Kai is your boyfriend. Is that true?" she asks as she blows her nose into the tissue.

I hesitate. I don't want to lie, and technically this bet made us a couple, so I say, "Yes, something like that. It's complicated."

She gives me an odd look. "He seems very nice."

I smile. "He is nice."

"Does he treat you like you're the most important person in the world to him?"

I consider that for a moment. So far he's been very kind, and protective of me—all because of some misplaced belief he owes it to me. The man doesn't date, doesn't want a girlfriend and I guess anyone can keep up the sweet, caring persona for a month.

"It's fairly new," I tell her. "But so far he's been great."

"I think he's cute," she says and I grin.

"I do too," Then I tease, "You're not going to try to steal him, are you?"

She frowns. "No, I'm not like that. I don't steal a guy another girl already likes." My gut clenches at that. while I'm here trying to help her, her words remind me that Bree has a huge crush on Kai, and he doesn't even know it. It would be horrible if I fell for him when she's been pining all this time.

What the heck am I even saying? I am not going to fall for Kai. We know the boundaries of this relationship. Brody comes back with the chips and drinks, and Sam smiles at him as he hands hers over.

"That was very nice of you, Brody." He shrugs it off and I like that. He doesn't need credit for a good deed. "Do you two want to hang out in here for a bit while you have your snacks?"

Brody nods eagerly, no doubt wanting to spend more time with his crush, and Sam agrees.

"When you're feeling better, come back to the dance. Is there any song you'd like the DJ to play? I can put in a request."

Brody pipes up and asks for a slow dance and I try to keep the grin from my face. "You got it."

I walk back into the dance, do a quick sweep of the kids laughing and hanging out, and make sure there's no kissing in the corner before I turn back to Kai, who is laughing at something Mila just said to him. Well, isn't that just sweet.

Come on, Jami, you have no right to be jealous.

I step up to them and before I can stop myself, I go up on my toes and press my lips to Kai's. I'm sure our kiss on my front steps has already made the rounds around our community, so what can this hurt?

Kai zeroes in on me, his eyes dark and curious as one hand slides around my waist. "Missed me, did you?" he asks, falling into the role of boyfriend.

"I just appreciate you helping out tonight."

"Did you get everything straightened out? Actually, it looks like you did," he says as he looks over my shoulder and I turn to see Brody and Sam laughing as they walk into the room. I exhale, happy that I was able to make the night a little easier for Sam.

"Crisis averted," I say, and note the way Mila is glaring at me. "Mila, if you're going to stay, do you mind taking over here, and I'll show Kai around?"

"Fine," she grumbles, and I put my arm through Kai's and lead him to the lobby. "What was that?" he asks when we're alone. Is he angry? No, he can't be, he's smiling and shaking his head.

"What?" I ask all innocently.

"You can't be jealous of Mila."

"No, of course not," I say quickly, feeling foolish for my actions. "We're just pretending and I thought that's what I should do at that moment."

He laughs out loud. "I'm not into high school girls, Jami."

"I never said you were, and I know what kind of girls you like."

"Do you now?" he challenges. "Who have you seen me with?"

"I just mean the puck bunnies, and cheerleaders. I saw the way they were all looking at you in the pub last night."

"You do realize you're a puck bunny, right?" he asks, and it takes me by surprise.

I frown and inch back, not really liking the term, because it holds negative connotations. "What, no."

"Jami, you *were* dating the captain of the hockey team, and went to all the games." The fact that he used *were* doesn't go unnoticed. He really considers Theo and I broken up and I guess I do too. Maybe that's the only way Theo will see what he had when he was with me. Maybe he'll covet what he can't have. Jeez, do I really want that? "That actually makes you head bunny."

"But I only started going to games after we started dating, and I don't party with the team afterward."

He clenches down on his jaw. "You should be." He steps closer, puts his finger under my chin and lifts my face until our eyes meet. "You just said I was into puck bunnies."

"Right."

"And I just told you, you are a puck bunny."

"Okay, maybe I now am. I'll concede that."

He grins at me and as I stare up at him, his gaze drops to my suddenly dry lips. Wait, is he saying he's into me?

KAI

“See you next week,” Jami says as the last of the kids exit the building and climb into their parent's cars. I follow her out into the cooler night, and an uneasy quiver goes through me as I take in the dark, overcast sky. Metal jingles as she locks up behind us and drops the key into a box.

“That was fun,” I say, and while I didn't mind it, the fun part was when she surprised me with a kiss. I get there's an attraction between us, even though I really don't want there to be, and it's kind of an ego boost to know she couldn't help but act on it too. She's officially broken up with douche bag, so it doesn't mean we can't. We just shouldn't. Mainly because I don't get involved and also, I have no doubt she'll go back to the guy who treats her like shit. Why does she stay with someone like that? Could it be because she doesn't feel she has any self-worth, stemming from the belief that she was only born to save her brother?

Maybe you should show her she has worth, Kai.

Jesus, what am I saying? I can't get involved. What if I got close to her only to…lose her. I can't go through that again.

"You liked it enough to do it again?" she asks and hugs herself.

"Where's your coat?"

"I accidently left it inside and I guess I could ask you the same. You never wear one."

"I run hot, remember." I shift from one foot to the next, happily uncomfortable, because that's what I deserve. "You said so yourself."

"Yeah, you do," she mumbles and I throw my arm around her shoulder and pull her in, offering my body warmth. We walk back to her place and the street is fairly quiet, and dark.

"The base is quite the party town on a Saturday night, huh?"

"Not much going on. I'm sure there's a party at Busters. Want to go there?"

Busters is the one and only local pub in Greenwood, and I wouldn't go near it with a ten-foot hockey stick, not just because it's a dive bar where fights regularly break out, but because I'm from Middleton and I wouldn't be welcomed. I don't need any kind of fighting interfering with my hockey. In fact, I don't need anything interfering with it, a girlfriend included. By rights, I should be back in Halifax at the rink, practicing, or re-watching games. Although I would like to see my folks and help out in the vineyard. It's actually one of the things that brings me joy, even though I don't deserve any kind of happiness in my life.

"No thanks," I grumble, a little angry with myself for this trip.

"I guess I should get you home, huh?"

"Yup."

She pulls her phone out and checks the time. "What time do you want to head back to the city tomorrow?"

"If you're not in a hurry, I'd prefer afternoon, that way I can spend the morning helping in the vineyard. My parents hire out, but they can always use an extra pair of hands and I've gotten quite good at picking over the years. I've been doing it for as long as I can remember."

"Oh really? Well, if you need all the hands you can get." She holds her hands up. "I have two right here."

"Yeah?"

"Sure." We reach her house and I follow her to the front door. "I could come by first thing in the morning."

"Or...you could grab your things and come stay the night."

She spins and looks at me. "You want me to stay the night?"

"I don't mean stay with me in my room or anything like that." I snort like that's the most ridiculous idea in the world, and while it is, I still like the sound of it. "We have spare bedrooms."

There's an eager kind of excitement in her eyes. "Honestly, Kai, I would love to see the property and the winery. I've only seen pictures of the weddings there, and that big, gorgeous fireplace you have out back."

"Then it's settled." I glance over my shoulders. "I don't like the idea of you being on the roads late at night driving home by yourself anyway. Especially when it looks like it could rain."

"Worried about me, Ward?"

"Yup." I really wish I didn't care. Caring leads to pain. But I can't seem to help it with her and it goes deeper than me feeling responsible because I won her in a bet. "The bet, remember?"

"I remember," she says and opens the front door.

Delicious smells come from the kitchen and her mother calls out, "I have some leftover lasagna if you guys want some."

Jami glances at me. "Hungry?"

"Yeah, but man, if you guys keep feeding me like this, I'll keep returning like the neighborhood cat."

She laughs at that and we make our way into the kitchen. Her mother grabs two plates and sets them out. "Your father isn't back yet. He got tied up at work."

"Darn. I'm actually going to spend the night at the vineyard with Kai." I don't miss the way her mother raises her brow. "I'm going to help them pick grapes in the morning. A thank you to Kai for helping out tonight."

"Maybe you can stop in tomorrow before you head to the city. Why don't you two go wash up and I'll serve you up some dinner?"

"I have to grab some clothes too." She steps into the hall and points to the bathroom just down the hall. "I'll run up and grab some things and be right back." She snatches her bag from where I left it near the front door, and instead of heading down the hall, I follow her to the stairs and she glances at me over her shoulder. "What are you doing?"

I gesture with a nod to the upstairs. "I want to see your room."

She laughs. "Why?"

I shrug. "No reason."

She shakes her head, turning to face me. "You're a strange man, Kai."

"That's one of the nicer things people from this town have called me." As soon as the words leave my mouth she frowns and puts her hand on my arms. "I'm sorry about Theo—I mean, my boyfriend. He never should have—"

"It's okay, and he's not your boyfriend, remember?"

"Right, my ex-boyfriend," she clarifies.

Something inside me gives, softens and I put my hand on her shoulder, and hold her before she can turn. My gaze drops to her mouth as she wets her lips. *Do not kiss her, Kai.* "Jami," I begin. "You don't have to do this—"

"I want to do this," she says, her voice filled with a new kind of conviction.

"If you want to go back to him."

"What do I have to do to make you understand that we're doing this, Kai? I'm in it for the month."

I briefly close my eyes and take a breath. "You don't want to know," I say, and turn her, giving her a nudge to set her into motion before I do something I can only regret. I work to keep my eyes off her ass as we climb the stairs and I stand in the hall when she enters her bedroom.

She holds her hands out. "This is it. Pretty sparse, actually. I brought a lot of my things to my place in the city." She opens a drawer and pulls out a few pieces of clothing and stuffs them into a bag. She grabs a brush from her dresser.

"Bring old clothes for picking tomorrow."

"Right." She goes to her closet and pulls out some sweats, shoving them into the bag as well. "All set," she says and comes toward me. I move to the side to let her pass and she walks to the bathroom. "You can wash up with me in here."

I step into the small space with her and she turns on the water. I reach for the soap dispenser and squirt it into her hands and then mine. I breathe in the cucumber scent. "Is this why you always smell like cucumbers?" I ask.

"I do not smell like cucumbers," she blurts out. "Besides, I remember you telling me I tasted sweet." I catch her gaze in the mirror and note the pink blotches on her cheeks. Is she blushing?

"I said you tasted sweet." I lean into her, putting my nose near her neck and inhale. "But you smell like cucumbers. It just so happens I love cucumbers."

She gives me an odd look, like she's working something out in her brain. Is it because I keep telling her I love things about her. "Actually, my shampoo has mint and cucumbers in it."

"See? I was right."

She laughs and lathers her hands. I do the same and when we both put them under the water at the same time, and our hands touch and linger, I hold her gaze in the mirror. Her skin is so fucking soft, I can't help but take her hands in mine. I glance down, and entwine my fingers in hers, rubbing the soap in soft circles over her palm and then sliding my thick finger between hers, to clean all the deep crevices.

My cock instantly thickens as we touch, and I note her breathing has changed, and I steal a glance at her to see her chest rise and fall a bit quicker. Fuck, what am I doing? I'm about to pull away when she starts touching me, running her fingers over mine and cleaning me in return. Her touch seeps under my skin and travels all the way to my thickening dick, which I can't hide in my jeans.

Even though my hands are soapy, I slide one around her neck, and dip my head to press my lips to hers. Her soft moan encourages me, and when she shifts her body to face me, putting her hands around my back, I press my palm to her backside and pull her against my erection.

I groan into her mouth as she moves against me and it's a goddamn good thing her mother is downstairs or I'd strip her bare right here in this bathroom and put my cock in her.

"Jami," I whisper. "Fuck."

"Kai," she murmurs back, her hands sliding under my shirt and skimming over my back. A hard quiver goes through me. I like her touch so goddamn much it's scary, because I don't want to like anything anymore. I don't deserve to feel good.

"Lasagna is on the table," her mother yells from downstairs, and we instantly break apart, both of us breathing hard. "I have to run next door. You two have fun picking grapes tomorrow, and we'll hopefully see you tomorrow before you head back."

Jami and I continue to stare at each other, the water running in the sink. The door closes downstairs, and I shut the water off, pick her up and set her on the sink. She widens her legs, grabs my shirt and pulls me back to her.

"Jami," I murmur. "We shouldn't..."

"I know," is all she says before she parts her lips, opening for me, and just like that, I'm a goner.

"Jesus." I kiss her harder this time, our tongues playing and tangling as I taste the depths of her. "So sweet," I murmur into her mouth. Her hands race over my chest, her fingers touching, tracing my muscles, which jump as she explores them. I tug her to the edge of the counter and press my cock to the warm juncture between her legs. She moves against me, rubbing herself on my hard cock.

Two days ago if someone told me I'd be dry humping Jami in her parents bathroom, I would have told them they were crazy, yet here I am, and I'm the crazy one. The downstairs door opens again, and some part of my brain registers it. Is her mother back? Or maybe her father is home?

I inch back and take in her lust-imbued eyes. "I, we…"

She nods like she can't find her words and swallows. I point to the door. "We should probably."

She nods again and I put my arms around her and lift her, letting her body slide down the length of me until her feet hit the floor. I bite back a groan as she presses against my cock, and I inch back, needing to tame the beast before we make our way to the kitchen.

She glances at her damp hair in the mirror. "Slippery," is all she mutters as she runs her hand along the back of her neck.

Slippery.

God, kill me now.

I take a couple of deep breaths as she grabs a towel to dry her hands. She passes it to me and I do the same. Without words, we leave the bathroom and when we reach the top of the stairs, Claire is walking back to the door.

"Forgot my pattern," she explains, holding it up. She disappears out the door again, closing it with a thud.

I glance at Jami. "Good thing she came back when she did, otherwise..."

"Yeah, good thing," she agrees, but as we stand there staring at each other, I'm pretty sure neither of us truly think that.

JAMI

Even though it would have been much quicker to take the highway to Middleton, Kai asked if I'd take the old road to his place. I didn't ask why, because I'm pretty sure it might have something to do with his accident, and that stretch of highway likely brings up way too many bad memories. I don't want him to revisit those old demons tonight. But damn, being in this car with him, in close confines after that mind-numbing kiss, is pretty much driving me insane. I honestly can't believe we did that, or that I blatantly pressed myself against his big, thickening cock.

What the heck was I thinking?

Oh right, I wasn't.

I glance at the dark sky and take in all the twinkling stars. It looked like rain earlier and I'm happy to see that the clouds have moved on. I don't much like driving in the rain.

"Your parents won't mind me staying?" I ask as I glance his way, admiring his strong profile.

He stretches his large hands out and fists them, only to open his fists and stretch his fingers out again, like he's not sure what to do with himself. "Nope, they'll be happy for the extra hands tomorrow."

Don't think about his hands, Jami. Especially don't think about how good they felt on your body.

I swallow hard, and he takes the cap off his water bottle and hands it to me. "Thanks." I take a drink and pass it back. He gulps some down before recapping it. As we drive through Middleton both of us lost in our thoughts, I point to the strip mall. "Look, the Halloween store is back."

"Oh yeah." He leans forward and looks out my window. "Maybe we can stop in there and get you a costume tomorrow."

"We could I suppose, but I'm sure the one in the city is back and opened by now. It's much bigger."

Don't think about bigger.

Great, now I'm thinking about what was bigger less than an hour ago. I swallow hard and then I sneeze.

"Allergies?" he asks.

"I think so." I glance at him. "Actually, I've been doing more sneezing since I've been around you."

"You allergic to me, Nichols?"

"It's possible," I tease and flick on my signal as I approach the long drive leading to his grand vineyard. The backyard is lit up, and music fills the air. My eyes go wide. "Do you think there's a wedding going on?"

"Seems like it."

"Want to crash it?"

He laughs at that. "You're going to get me into trouble one of these days."

I frown and ease into the big parking lot that's filled with cars. "That's a no."

"That's a no, but it doesn't mean we can't watch, or have cake and drinks."

I turn the car off and put my keys in my purse. "Cake, yum." I peer up at the grand building, with all the twinkling lights. "Do you think it could be someone we know getting married?"

"Possible, but people come from all over Nova Scotia." He opens his door. "Want a tour?"

I nod eagerly and jump from the car. Kai grabs our bags and puts them over his shoulder and as I watch him, my legs go a little weak. This is a dream, right? No way can I possibly be at Kai Ward's vineyard, about to sleep at his big estate.

"Coming?"

"Yeah."

He angles his head. "You spaced for a second there."

"I guess I can't quite believe I'm here." He puts his arm around me, and we start toward the big wooden building which pays homage to the heritage of agriculture buildings in the Annapolis Valley. At least that's what I read.

"It's so gorgeous Kai."

"There's over fifty acres of vines planted along the shores of the Minas Basin." He points. "Way off in the distance you can see Cape Blomidin. Have you ever hiked it?"

"No, never. I'd like to someday."

"Eight-point four kilometers in. Eight-point four kilometers out. But it's definitely something to see. Maybe we'll do it sometime."

"Maybe," I answer, knowing that time will never come. We're both busy with school and sports and I'm sure we won't be able to pack a hike in, not before our thirty days are over.

What if you extended it?

Good Lord, what am I even saying?

We step up to the gorgeous, architectural building, and I admire the big glass double doors, which have fake barn style doors flanking them. Kai pulls open the doors and the first thing I notice is the romantic ambiance.

My phone pings, and Kai arches a brow. I pull it from my pocket. "It's Mom checking to make sure we got here okay." I quickly text her back to let her know everything is fine. I tuck it away and we step further inside the beautiful winery, and I take it all in.

He stops outside an archway. "In the winter, the wedding dinners are held in this room." I glance in and see a long oaken table, with maybe thirty chairs, and the table is staged with all the plates, glasses, vases and flowers. Gorgeous chandeliers hang from the ceiling.

"Wow, I might want a winter wedding just to use this room," I tell him.

"You say that, but wait until you see the set-up outside in the vineyard." We walk toward the back of the building, and he glances into a room—I guess it's the wine store, considering all the bottles on the shelves—and waves to the woman at the counter. He pushes the doors open and I'm presented with a high, stone fireplace. The smell of fresh wood burning fills the air and I step up to it, and feel the heat on my body as I breathe in.

"It's perfect," I murmur. Actually, everything about this vineyard is perfect, absolutely gorgeous and for a moment, I almost laugh. I used to think about Theo and I getting married—not that we ever talked about it—and while this is the perfect place, there is no way we could have our wedding here, considering how much he hates Kai, and vice versa.

"You want to get married, Jami?"

I spin and find Kai staring at me, his head dipped, his hands in his pockets. "What?" I blurt out.

His brow furrows for a second, no doubt confused by my outburst, and then laughs. "I don't think that came out right. I wasn't asking if you wanted to marry me. I was asking if someday you wanted to get married, to someone."

It's possible I do, but I'm not sure anyone wants to marry me. I turn from him quickly, hoping he didn't see the sudden pain on my face. I hold my hands out to the fire, pretending to warm myself, but I'm not sure there is anything to lessen the chill that always resides inside me.

"Hey, I'm sorry."

"What are you sorry for?" I ask, trying to sound as if I don't have a care in the world and while we don't really know each other well, I did open up to him a bit about why I was born, and Kai is a very smart guy.

"My question upset you."

Despite the music in the distance, his boots sound on the stone floor as he closes the small distance between us, and I quiver as he puts his arms around me and pulls me toward him until my back is pressed against his hard chest. His heart beats so strong it vibrates through me.

He holds me tight and long, so long that something inside me breaks. "It's just...my ex was quick to let me go in a bet, as you know, and there's...there's a part of me that believes, I'm just not that important...to anyone. That I'm not ever seen, or have any value."

He puts his mouth near my ear. "That's not true, Jami."

I nod, even though I don't believe him. "Thanks." That one word comes out sounding flat.

"I'm sorry."

"You already said that."

"I'm sorry that betting on you made you feel like a commodity or that you had no value."

"You had your reasons."

"Yes, I did and maybe some of those reasons had nothing at all to do with your ex, and I bet on you because I saw the value in you."

Is he serious? Is he saying he bet on me because he wanted me, or is he saying all this just to make me feel better?

Is it making you feel better, Jami?

Yeah, it is, so does it really matter the reason behind his words? I guess it could matter, if he was truly into me.

"Kai?" His name hovers in the air, as someone in the distance calls out to him and he backs away from me. I turn to see a man and woman coming our way. Kai goes so stiff and still, I'm sure if I touched him with my pinkie finger, he'd snap in two. I have no idea what's going on, but he's upset, so I step up to him and put my hand on his back, offering warmth and support.

"Hi," he manages to croak out. "What...what are you guys doing here?"

The man gestures toward the canopy set up on the slopes. "Andrea and Caleb's wedding."

"You remember Andrea? Coop's cousin." the woman asks, and while her smile is big, and genuine, there's an uneasy nervousness about her.

"Yes."

He lowers his head and the couple's eyes turn my way. "Hi," I say quickly. "I'm Jami Nichols. Kai's...uh." Do I say girlfriend? I don't know these people and they've upset Kai and we're boyfriend and girlfriend, but not really. This is all so messed up.

"We know each other from school," Kai explains quickly.

My hand falls from his back, and my heart pinches tight at the coolness in his tone. I take a small step back, trying to catch my breath, to figure out what the heck is going on. One second he's holding me and telling me I have value, the next he's as cold as a Nova Scotia winter.

"Right, we know each other from school," I finally manage to get out as the man and woman continue to stare at me. Okay, so we're pretending to be a couple because of the bet, but now I'm just someone he knows from school. How messed up is that? As messed up as Kai, I guess and it's a good reminder that I'm simply a means to an end for him, and vice versa, of course.

"It's nice to meet a friend of Kai's." They hold their hands out and I have no choice but to shake them as they introduce themselves as Candace and Gerald Cooper.

It's nice to meet you both," I say numbly.

"Feel free to come and join the party," Candace says, and smiles at Kai, like she's trying to offer her comfort. "I'm sure Andrea would love to see you."

"I...uh...haven't even seen Mom or Dad yet."

"Okay, well afterward, if you want to join, you're more than welcome," she says.

Gerald looks over his shoulder. "I saw your parents around here earlier."

Candace smiles. "Well, we won't keep you. You two have a great night and we hope to see more of you both."

They leave and Kai continues to stand perfectly still. I give him a minute and turn to the fire, hoping it will help with the chill still lingering around Kai.

I finally ask, "Kai, are you okay?"

"No, not really," he whispers so quietly I have to strain to hear.

I step up to him, and his legs don't seem to work all that well as I lead him to one of the benches near the fire. "Do you want to talk about it?"

He sits, plants his elbows on his knees and covers his face with his hands. "No."

"Okay." I just sit there quietly with him, and when a server comes by, she seems to think we're part of the wedding celebration, and holds a tray of champagne out to us. I accept two glasses. I take a much-needed drink of the bubbly and set Kai's down on the small table beside him.

After a very long moment, he lifts his flute, downs the fluid in one gulp and says, "They were...the Coopers."

I realize that because they introduced themselves. But exactly who they are is still out of my grasp. I take a sip of champagne and search my memory. That's when the pieces of the puzzle fall into place. Candace and Gerald Cooper. Coop. Kai's best friend. The one who died in the accident. I honestly don't know much about it. I was sheltered from everything in high school, and while I heard talk about it, the names never really registered.

"I'm sorry, Kai," I murmur and put my arm around him. We sit in silence for a long time, and I leave him with his thoughts as music from the wedding fills the night air. I struggle being quiet at times, as I'd like to say something to slay his demons, and as a social work student, I'm usually pretty good at helping. I'm not sure he wants that from me, though, which is maybe why I'm at a loss for words. One thing I do know is that while Kai is still in terrible pain, it doesn't seem like the Coopers are angry or blame him.

Footsteps sound on the floor, and Kai stands. "Let's go out to the vineyard." I eye him. He can't be serious. As if reading my expression he clarifies, "Not to the wedding, let's just go walk the rows in the vineyard."

I glance at the big sweater I'm wearing. "It's warm here by the fire but the night air is cold and you should probably grab a sweater."

"I don't want one. Come on, we can drop our bags off at the house first."

I nod, and he takes my hand in his, holding it so tight, I'm worried he's going to crack my bones, but I don't complain. We follow a lit path along the side of the winery, and off in the distance I take in the wedding guests dancing under a canopy. It looks gorgeous.

As we reach the top of a hill, his family's house rises up in the distance. "It's a mansion," I murmur. He doesn't say anything. Instead, he guides me to the house, opens the door, drops our bags inside, and closes it again.

"Are we going to go say hi to your parents?"

"We'll see them later. They're probably overseeing the wedding. I'm sure the Coopers probably told them they ran into us, so they know I'm home."

"Okay."

He takes my hand in his and leads me along another path that takes us up another hill to another vineyard. It's much quieter here, the music fading to dim melody. We walk past a big barn, and he lets my hand go. I instantly miss his warmth.

"Hang on." He ducks inside, only opening the door enough to squeeze in and out, which is strange, and comes out with a blanket, checking to make sure the door is securely shut behind him. He tosses the blanket over his shoulder. It's not a jacket, but at least it will keep him warm. He takes my hand again and we walk through the vineyard and he's mostly quiet, but does explain the variety of grapes we're walking beside, which I find rather interesting.

We reach the end of the row to where there's a clearing and he spreads the blanket out. "Have a seat," he says and as I sit, he snags a few grapes from the closest vine. He drops down next to me, and I snuggle close, wanting to keep him warm. He holds a grape out to me.

"Open." I'm about to reach for the grape, but he pulls it back. "Hey, it's not like you're a feeding virgin."

"What?" I ask quickly.

"I mean you let me feed you twice, so what does a third time hurt? Besides, grapes taste better when someone feeds them to you."

"Yeah, sure," I say with a laugh and even though I don't believe him, I open my mouth. He puts the grape on my tongue and flavor bursts in my mouth as I bite into it. "Mmm," I moan.

He lays back on the blanket and I drop down beside him. We stare at the stars and I search for constellations. We're both quiet for a long time.

He finally breaks the silence and asks, "I guess you figured it out, huh?"

"Yes."

He turns toward me. "Thanks for just sitting with me." He takes my hand, brings it to his mouth and kisses it. I turn to face him and take in the pain on his face.

"Whatever you need, Kai."

"Yeah?" he asks, his voice an octave deeper as he tucks my hair behind my ear.

"Yeah," I respond, and when his gaze drops to my mouth, I'm pretty sure I know exactly what he needs. I think I might need it too.

Baaa....

KAI

"What the hell?" I roll over and come face to face with Cotton, one of the many sheep on the farm. How do I know it's Cotton? Because she's a damn con artist, always pretending she's asleep in the barn, tricking us all with her antics, when in reality she's plotting her escape the second we leave. But maybe this is a sign that I shouldn't be messing around with Jami on a blanket in the vineyard, or anywhere else for that matter. "How did you get out? I shut the door securely behind myself."

"Um, are you talking to a sheep?"

"Jami, meet Cotton. The con."

"Why do you call her that?" Jami sits up as I push to my feet.

"You saw me close the barn door, right?" I ask as I run my fingers through my hair, trying to figure out how she gets out all the time.

"Yeah, I did."

"I checked on her before I left, and she was pretending to be asleep."

"Oh, so that's why you were squeezing in and out." She frowns. "Wait, how does a sheep pretend to be asleep?" Her eyes narrow and she looks at me like I might have taken one too many pucks to the head.

"She lays there and doesn't move, because she's conning us." Just then Cotton baa's again and she pushes her head against me. I rub her head the way she likes it and she baa's some more.

"Maybe you should have named her Fleece."

"Noooo," I groan and shake my head as I jump to my feet. "A sheep named Fleece. You didn't just say that."

She chuckles. "Come on. A sheep that cons you, bamboozles you. Fleece is the perfect name."

"Jami, no. Just...no," I tease, and reach out to help her to her feet.

She crinkles her nose. "That bad?"

"Jami, babe." I give her a playful groan. "That was so bad."

"Hello, Cotton," Jami says and rubs her back. "She's so soft. I didn't realize you had a sheep."

"One of many," I tell her.

"Do you have her sheared?"

"Yes, and we sell or use the wool."

"How do you use it?" Before I can answer she says, "Do you knit with it?" She pokes me, amusement on her face. "Like you, personally."

I shrug. "Yeah, sometimes. My grandmother taught me to knit when I was a wee boy. My grandmother was Scottish," I tell her, explaining my use of the word wee.

Her mouth gapes open. "I can't believe you can knit." She stares up at me, her face full of admiration. "I had no idea you were a man of so many talents."

I shrug like it's nothing. "What good Nova Scotia farmer doesn't knit?"

I reach for the blanket and put my hand on the small of Jami's back to set her into motion. Cotton naturally follows. She's such a social sheep.

"I always thought that was just a myth," she laughs.

"Nope. Do you remember Tanner Bang from our team? He's actually from Minnesota. He was fascinated by the socks I made."

She shakes her head. "I don't remember him. I didn't really go to the games until..." She lets her words fall off and I'm glad she didn't say douche bag's name.

"Oh, well he's in the NHL and plays for the Boston Bucks. I taught him how to knit. He loves it."

"I actually think that's cool. Maybe you could teach me."

"Yeah, sure." We make our way back to the barn, and I find the door cracked open. "How does she do it?" I ask. I pull the door open wider, and give her a little slap. "In you go, Cotton."

She baa's at me and tromps inside, dropping down in her favorite spot. "Go to sleep, for real this time." I shut the door and triple check that it's closed tightly. I do not need to be cock blocked by a sheep twice in one night.

Not that I plan to do anything with Jami. In her bathroom, or here in the vineyard. Huge mistakes. Not going to happen again. Fine, it's true I so much as admitted I wanted her when she told me she felt unworthy, but that doesn't mean I have to act on it.

"We should head up to the house. It's getting late and we have an early morning."

"Okay," she agrees, and this time I don't take her hand. We walk in silence and as we approach the house, the wedding music reaches our ears. I open the door and call out to my parents, but there's no answer.

"I guess you won't meet them until morning." She nods and I pick our bags up. "Come on, I'll show you to your bedroom."

I head up the stairs and her footsteps are light as she follows me. I glance over my shoulder to make sure she's actually coming. Maybe after the dry humping in the bathroom and the kissing in the vineyard she's changed her mind about all this, and that would be for the best.

I take in the way she's glancing over the rail into the living room. "Your house is beautiful and huge for just three people."

"Coop practically…" I let my words fall off. The place has felt so empty without his presence here. My heart squeezes so tight for a second that I can't breathe. I grip the handrail as my entire body freezes.

"He spent a lot of time here, didn't he?" she asks quietly and puts her hand over mine.

I swallow against my tight throat. I open my mouth, not sure my words will even come but then manage to reply. "Yeah, we were very close." I pinch my eyes shut for a second, and when

I do the vision of my best friend beside me, mangled and dead in the passenger seat sends a wave of grief through my body. "We were brothers, you know," I whisper, my voice shaking.

"That's really nice, Kai. To have had someone who meant so much to you."

"Yeah, well." I stand up straighter and call on the anger. Sometimes it's the only way I can get through these moments. "The key word is *had*. I don't have him now," I say harshly, even though she doesn't deserve that from me, not when she's so caring and supportive. But anger is my go to emotion, and I don't seem to have any control over it.

She doesn't retreat from me. Instead, she says, "I'm sorry." Her voice is low, quiet and sad—for me, for my dead best friend.

I drop the bags outside the spare bedroom and turn to her. "No, I'm sorry. I didn't mean to snap at you like that. Some-times..." I snort out a laugh that holds zero humor. "More like 'all the time', it still hurts."

She nods. "I can imagine."

I wave my hand. "This is your room."

She glances inside. "Was this where he slept?"

"No, he had another room down the hall. It really hasn't been touched since... A lot of his stuff is still in there, but I don't go near it." I pick her bag up and carry it to her bed. I point across the hall. "I'm across from you, and the bathroom is to your right. My parents' room is on the other wing of the house, so this bathroom is just for us." I pick a piece of grass from her hair. "You can shower if you want."

"I think I will. I'm chilly from laying on the ground."

"Hang on." I disappear and come back with a pair of knitted socks. "Wear these to bed. They'll keep you warm."

She laughs as she takes them from me, turning them over in her hands to examine the stitch. "I love these. Did you make them?" I nod. "Now I love them even more. Thank you." She goes up on her toes and presses her lips to mine, and I fist my hands at my sides before I wrap them around her and pull her to me. I want to. I really fucking want to, but I can't get close to her. I can't get close to anyone. If I did and I lost her...

"Goodnight," I whisper, and leave her room. I bend and pick up my bag. "If you need anything, you know where to find me." I pull her door shut and let out a harsh breath. I really need to get my shit together and I think the only way I can do that is by ending this thing once and for all. After we head back tomorrow, I'll let her know it's over and that maybe her brother should invite the hockey team from Kingston for his party. Granted, Brad isn't on that team, and I get he wants to hook up with him, but he'll have to find a way outside of his party.

I push off the door, toss my bag into my room and dart to the bathroom to clean up before bed. Once I'm done, I go into my bedroom, strip down to my boxers, and throw myself down on the mattress. I grab my phone and find an old hockey game to watch, anything to keep my mind off the woman next door and what I want to do to her with my cock.

I suck in a breath as her door opens, and grin when she sneezes. Maybe she really is allergic to me. The bathroom door clicks shut and the shower turns on. I set my phone down and roll over. The air is cool and I let it chill my body as I close my eyes, willing sleep to come.

The next thing I know, a sneeze wakes me and I glance at the clock to find it's the middle of the night. Maybe I should check in on Jami and see if she needs some allergy medication. I'm sure we must have some in the bathroom. Has she slept at all?

I slide off the bed and walk to my door. I open it and walk across the hall. I stand still and listen for sound, and when none comes, I assume she's fallen back to sleep. I'm about to turn when her door opens.

"Oh," she gasps when she finds me standing there. "What are you doing?"

"I heard you sneezing and came to check on you. I thought you might need something."

Her gaze drops and that's when I realize I'm only in my boxers, and she's dressed in a T-shirt and loose-fitting pajama pants. I know that look isn't supposed to be sexy, but damn, the way those pants hang low on her hips, exposing the soft skin of her abdomen—instant boner. Not only that, she's in the wool socks I gave her and looks absolutely fucking adorable.

"Jami."

"Yeah," she answers sounding breathless, her chest rising and falling quickly. So is mine.

I reach out, and lightly rub my thumb over the inside of her wrist. "You just came out of your bedroom and found me standing in the hall."

"Uh huh," she says, clearly confused.

I lean into her and dip my head. "You're not running and screaming."

Her warm breath, which is coming faster now, warms my skin. "You're right, I'm not."

I take a small step toward her and this time I don't smell her cucumber and mint fragrance. No, this time I smell my body wash on her. "Why is that?"

"I...uh...you were right when you said you thought I might need something," she murmurs.

"Allergy medication?"

She shakes her head no, and I gulp as her gaze falls down the length of me, stopping to examine my growing cock. While one part of me wants to lock myself in the bedroom until she goes back to the city, the other part of me, the part thickening between my legs, is having nothing to do with running away from her.

"Jami," I murmur, and put one arm around her and pull her against my body. Her softness against my hardness is excruciatingly sensual, and I bend down to capture her mouth with mine. She kisses me back, her tongue seeking and playful.

While I still have one working brain cell, and before I can talk myself out of this, I pick her up and she wraps her legs around me as I carry her to my room. I kick the door shut and walk to the bed, and drop to my knees, setting her on the mattress.

That's when that one brain cell kicks in and I inch back. Her eyes go wide, and I'm pretty sure she thinks I'm having second thoughts. With the way I've been so hot and cold with her, it's no wonder.

She reaches out and puts her warm palms on my face. "Kai?"

"You were coming out of your room." Maybe she was running away. No, she was still in her pajamas. "Were you going somewhere?"

She relaxes a bit. "I actually had a tickle in my throat. I was going to get a drink of water from the bathroom faucet."

"Hang on." Boner still engaged and ready for launch, I rush down to the kitchen and grab two water bottles. I'm breathless by the time I get back. I crack one bottle and hand it to her. "Still allergic to me?"

She takes a drink, sets the bottle on my nightstand and crooks her finger. "Let's find out."

I grin at her playfulness. "So, this is like one of those allergy tests, where they scratch your back, put on the allergen, and watch to see if it swells?"

"Are you going to scratch my back, Kai?"

"I'd have to scratch it and then lick it, you know, because I'm the allergen."

"Licking...licking is good," she tells me, her voice low and deep as she squirms and just seeing her so needy for me drives me wild.

"Are you going to scratch mine?" I ask.

"I want to, yes, but I don't need to." I angle my head, not understanding and she grins. "You're already swelling." She glances at my erection as it shamelessly tents my boxers and I grin, loving this playful side of her.

"I once heard that to overcome allergies, you just have to repeatedly expose yourself to that allergen to try to alter the persons immune response," I explain.

"It's called immunotherapy," she clarifies, and I love how smart she is. "You train your body to accept an allergen."

"So, what I'm hearing here, is that if you are allergic to me, we'll have to do this." I wave my hand over her quivering body. "A whole lot more."

She puckers her lips, insinuating in a teasing way that everything about this is unpleasant. "Seems that way."

"You realize I'm doing this to help you, right?"

She chuckles. "You're a good friend."

Her use of the word friend doesn't go unnoticed, and I'm surprised she'd call me that after I was so fucking rude when I called her someone I knew from school. But that thought is for later. I drop to my knees, and spread her legs to climb in between them. She cups my face again and kisses me. I breathe in her sweet smell and move my mouth to her neck, dying to taste every inch of her sweetness.

"Kai," she whispers and I move my mouth from her neck to her breasts, lightly rubbing my lips over the swells in her T-shirt. "Yes," she murmurs and her nipples pucker under my ministrations. She moves against me, cupping the back of my head as I slide my fingers under her top, and slide them up to grip her breasts. She moans in delight and lifts her arms above her head, encouraging me to rid her of her clothing. You don't have to ask me twice.

I grip the bottom of her shirt and peel it from her body, going back on my heels to admire her gorgeous breasts, which are pert and lush and beckoning my mouth. "Jami, babe…"

Her eyes glow with desire as I simply admire her. "Kai?"

There's confusion in her voice. "Yeah, babe?"

"What are you doing?"

"I'm just looking...enjoying. Do you have any idea how beautiful you are?"

Her shoulders curl in a bit. "No one has ever looked at me like you're looking at me right now."

"You don't like it?"

"I think it makes me feel both self-conscious, and desirable."

I work really hard not to think about her douche bag boyfriend and how he doesn't deserve her. But I understand now, knowing her history, that being liked by the popular guy was a real ego boost for her. Honestly, I've known douche bag for years, and Jami is a nice girl, not the kind he goes for. The more I think about it, the more I worry about his agenda.

"You are desirable. There isn't any other girl I want to be with, Jami." Goddammit, that scares the shit out of me so much I'm close to jumping to my feet and bailing, but stop when she smiles. I can't let her think I don't want her. I do, and I want to show her she's beautiful, worthy and has value outside of being born to save her brother.

"You want me, Kai?"

"Fuck yes, I do."

"Come show me."

I go up on my knees, and fall on top of her, kissing the fuck out of her mouth as I push my cock against her body. Yeah, there's no denying that I want her. The proof is pressing against her hot center and begging for more.

I slide down her body and take one gorgeous nipple into my mouth. I suck deeply, until she's writhing, moaning and wrapping her legs around my waist, her heels pressing into my ass and pushing me harder against her hot center.

I move against her, and goddammit, while this dry humping is fun, I need to be inside her. I slide down more, until my knees are back on the floor, and I grip her pajama pants. She goes up on her elbows and puts her legs on the floor in front of me. I check in with her. Just to make sure this is what she wants.

"Yes, please," she moans, and I start inching her pants down, slowly, to prolong the moment, even though I want to tear them from her hips and put my cock inside her. I expose the curve of her pelvic bone and I lean in and press my lips to her soft skin. I rake my teeth over her flesh and she whimpers and puts her hands on her stomach, her fingers following the path of my mouth. Her skin glistens from my wet mouth, and something about the sight of it excites me.

I tug her pants down until I see her damp dark curls and as I breathe in her sweet arousal, I realize that the second I put my mouth on her, the second I taste the depths of her sweetness, it might become my undoing.

So, what's your next move going to be, Kai?

With my pants hovering just below my sex, his eyes glued to my body, I go up higher on my elbows to see him. My God, I was right when I said no man has ever looked at me the way Kai does. But right now, I sense there's more going on. I sense a struggle. Because once we cross this line, we've crossed it. There's no coming back from that. I'm about to reach out to him, but stop when his shoulders relax and he slides his tongue from the bottom of my pussy to the top, using the soft blade to circle my engorged clit.

"Oh, God," I groan and fall back, grabbing a fistful of his sheet. "Kai..."

"Mmm," is all he murmurs in response as he buries his face between my legs and pleasures me like it's his damn job. Oh, how I want it to be.

His head lifts, his tongue no longer on me, and I hurry onto my elbows to see him. He grins up at me. "Swelling," he informs me, and runs his thumb over my aching clit. "So much swelling. Looks like you are allergic to me and I'm going to have to spend a lot of time trying to alter your response."

"Yes, it seems that way," I agree and lift my hips to bump my sex against his chin, encouraging him to get at it already. He laughs, and dives back in, sliding his hands under my backside to lift my pussy to his mouth like he's at a damn buffet, and I love it. Honestly, he could do this every day, and every day I'd swell for him.

The noises he's making, like giving me pleasure is a pleasure for him, astounds me just a little bit. I don't want to compare him to my ex. Heck, Theo is the only other guy I've been with and I just assumed that the way sex was with him was the way every couple experienced it. Sadly, I was mistaken, and to think this is what I've been missing out on.

"Kai, that feels so..." My words die an abrupt death as he slides a thick finger into me, finding a spot that shuts down my ability to think. "Ohmigod."

"Yeah, babe, you like that?"

He wiggles his finger, and licks at my clit and the only response I can find is a garbled moan of sheer appreciation. "You're so nice and wet. I can't wait to put my cock inside you."

While I want that right now, I don't want him to stop what he's doing either. I fall back on the bed and chant his name as he does the most delicious things between my legs. I move, shamelessly begging for...everything.

Another finger joins the first. "Oh," escapes my lips as he stretches me, and changes the pressure on my clit. His tongue sharpens and he laps at me as his fingers work their magic spell on my quaking body. "Please, don't stop."

"Not going to, babe. I want you to come all over my fingers and mouth."

Oh God, dirty talk. I'm not good at it, and up until this moment, I didn't even know I liked it. "I want that, Kai. I want to come on your face." I lift my head to sneak a peek at him, praying I didn't just sound like a fool, but when I meet his dark, intense eyes, it's clear I'm on to something. "Your face is wet from my juices," I add.

"Fuck me," he growls, and that's when my world turns upside down. He eats at me, devours me as he fucks me with his fingers, changing the pace and rhythm until my eyes roll back and I'm fisting the sheets so hard I'm ripping them off the bed. His sheer moan of bliss is what pushes me over the edge and my body succumbs to the pleasure, liquid happiness pouring from my body. He moans in delight, his tongue now circling my clit as my muscles clench around his thick fingers.

He shifts his body, his cock now pressing against my leg, and it's easy to tell he's in agony. Damned if I don't want to help with that, especially after he so carefully and thoroughly brought me to orgasm. I sit up and he lifts his head. I press my lips to his as my spasms subside and he slowly pulls his fingers from me.

"I think it's only fair that I subject your body to the same therapy."

He angles his head, waiting to hear more. I reach down and cup his cock through his boxers, and when I squeeze, his head falls back, a moan filling the air.

"Fuck, Jami," he growls as I stand, my wet sex bumping against his mouth. He sticks his tongue out to taste me again, and now I'm the one growling.

I touch his shoulder. "Come here."

He stands, and the second he does, I sink to my knees. I breathe on his cock through his boxers, and love the way the crown breaks through the band, peeking at me with it's one eye.

"So swollen," I murmur, as he grips my hair to move it off my shoulder. "I have no choice but to spend time here, Kai. If you're helping me, it's only right that I help you too." I blink up at him. "You do want that, don't you?"

"Jesus, yes, I want that," he blurts out and it brings a smile to my face. I love his enthusiasm, and while I'm sure he's like that with every girl, I'm not going to think about that. I'm just going to enjoy this moment and the allergy research we're conducting. It's fun, and I honestly can't remember the last time I had fun. No, that's not true. I had fun at the car wash, at our picnic, during the drive to the valley, and while visiting his vineyard. Okay, and yes, of course I had fun making out with him in my bathroom. Now, though, there are no clothes standing in our way and I plan to take full advantage of the lack of barriers.

Subjecting him to the same slow torture, I slowly tug on his boxers, exposing his cock little by little, even though I want to get a good look at it. Admire it really, as I take it into my hand and spend a moment just looking, like he did with me.

"Jami," he complains, and moves his hips forward, wanting my mouth on him sooner rather than later.

"Is there a problem?"

"You're killing me, babe. Please," he begs. "Put your mouth on me."

I have never heard a man plead before and I can't stand for him to be in pain, so I tug his boxers down to his thick thighs and free his beautiful, fat cock, which is erect and upright and inches from my mouth. I lick him from bottom to top and I'm rewarded with a tortured moan of pleasure.

"Is this what you want?"

He growls. "Yes, and a lot more of it if you want to take care of my swelling."

I grin and reposition myself, pulling on his cock so I can take it into my mouth. His pre-cum is warm and tangy on my tongue as I slide my tip around his crown to taste him. He moves his body, feeding me his cock. It slides to the back of my throat and I do my best to relax my throat so I don't choke.

His moans of joy thrill me and my body quivers, aching to feel him inside me. But I love what I'm doing and don't want to stop. That decision is taken away from me, when Kai bends, takes my arms and pulls me off his cock. I frown up at him, about to berate him, but the serious, intense look on his face fills me with a new kind of hunger for him.

He shoves his boxers to his ankles and kicks them off and I grow hotter between my legs. He turns us until the back of his knees hit the bed and I'm facing him. He sits down and puts his face to my stomach, breathing me in as he guides me to stand in front of his lap. He shifts and the sound of his nightstand drawer opening draws my attention. I stand on shaky legs for a second as he rips into the condom and sheathes himself with expert ease.

"Legs on either side of me," he commands softly, and I climb onto the bed, sitting on his lap, his thick cock parting my nether lips and pressing against my clit. I glance down to look at the way he's positioned us, and he grips my hips and lifts me up and down.

"Oh," I moan, my eyes opening wide and my nipples tightening as he stimulates my clit, and spreads my juices all over his cock. I move my body, riding him like a damn scratching post and I really don't care.

"Yeah, baby," he murmurs, putting his face between my breasts and pressing kisses to my skin. "I love that."

I'm not exactly sure what he's referring to, but I love all this too. He lets me rub myself until I'm moaning and close to a second release, then he grips my hips and holds me completely still. I moan and complain, wanting nothing more than to find release.

"Kai," I murmur, and knowing exactly what I need, he lifts my hips, and I go up on my knees. He positions me over his erect cock and I groan with happiness as his eyes meet mine and he pulls me down. "Kai," I say, and melt a little inside while my body gives way to warmth and need. Some deeper emotion I refuse to identify grips me as his dark eyes hold mine, like I'm his lifeline that allows himself to feel pleasure.

"Jami," he murmurs as he fills me completely, his crown pressing against my cervix and threatening to bring on a full body orgasm. Not that I really know what that feels like. I've only ever read about it. Being here with Kai, on his bed, his thick cock filling me, it's strangely beautiful, and...moving. I'm not sure why. Perhaps it's because he's unhurried, almost afraid to take his own pleasure as he gives it.

He stays perfectly still, seating his cock high inside me as he tilts his head up and holds my gaze. I stare back, neither of us needing to vocalize what we're feeling—and I'm not just talking about the physical feelings. He lightly touches my arms, a soft, gentle caress full of care, before he slides his hands around my back, spreading his fingers so that he's touching all of me as he pulls me to him, turning his head to the side as he places his cheek on my heart.

"You feel so good, Jami," he murmurs quietly, his voice hitching slightly.

"You do too," I tell him and he lifts his head, his eyes glossy as they search my face. I lean in and kiss him softly and when he moans it curls around my heart. I think there might be more going on here than just plain sex. I could be wrong, but I don't think so.

I squeeze my muscles around him and he sucks in a breath, grips my hips again and starts moving my body, lifting me up and down on his cock, like I weigh nothing, and maybe to him I don't. I put my hands on his shoulders, loving the strength in his muscles as he maneuvers me over his cock. I let him fuck me, let him take charge, because everything in the way he's touching me, lets me know how much he cares about my body, and I trust him with it.

"That's good," he grunts out as I grow slicker, my dripping wet pussy taking every inch he wants to give me. He changes the pace, pulling me down harder and harder, and the force against my cervix sends shudders through my entire body. I quake around him and he grunts. "Yeah Jami, just like that."

"My God, Kai. It's incredible," I tell him. I ride him and grind and give and take, wanting to give him the kind of pleasure he's giving me.

He gives a long, slow grunt, and moves his body so my clit grinds on his pelvis every time he thrusts into me. I open my mouth as my orgasm takes shape. "Kai."

"I know, babe, I know. I'm there too."

Just knowing that he's right there with me sends me over the edge and I let go. He growls as my hot juices pour over his pistoning cock, and I clench hard around him. He throws his head back, and grips my hips to still my movements as I continue to spasm. A second later, he thickens even more inside me and closes his eyes in bliss as he gives himself over to his own orgasm.

"Fuck," he murmurs, and takes big gulping breaths as he depletes himself.

I can't take my eyes off his face. The pleasure, the sheer ecstasy I see reflected there... I want to see it every time I close my eyes and think of him, which I suspect will be often. His breath is hot on my skin as he pants, and I run my hands through his damp hair. He puts his hands on either side of my face and kisses my mouth gently.

I'm about to tell him he was incredible, but before I can get the words out, I sneeze. He laughs, and reaches for the water bottle. "Take a drink. I really am beginning to believe you are allergic to me."

"Me too," I agree. "I can't remember the last time my allergies were so bad." I wiggle on his cock, and teasingly continue, "Looks like we'll have to do more of this."

He shakes his head, and something in his demeanor changes, becomes sad and stoic. "I need to get rid of the condom." He lifts me off his cock, and I sit on the side of the bed. "Be right back." I watch him hurry from the room, admiring his firm ass. A minute later, he comes back with tissues and a warm cloth.

He takes the bottle from my hand and puts it on the nightstand. "Lay back," he commands softly. I do as he asks and he cleans me up. The second the warmth hits my sex, it seeps through my skin and curls around my heart. What is it about his gentleness and sensitivity that gets to me? My God, I'm not falling for him, am I? I can't be. He has a girl back in the city who is in love with him and I can't be the one to come between them, and I broke up with Theo for one month. I agreed to this bet, this situation, because I had my own agenda. Are things changing for me? Do I not want what I thought I wanted just the other day?

Am I losing my mind thinking that what we just did wasn't just about sex?

He finishes cleaning me and disappears for a second. When he comes back, I'm gathering up my clothes. "Are you going back to your room?" he questions, and he's so somber—like what we'd just did was a mistake, and maybe it was—I can't tell if that's what he wants or not.

"I...I..."

He pushes his hair from his forehead. "You can sleep in here if you want."

"What do you want?" I ask, and suck in a breath as I wait for an answer.

His gaze goes from me, to the bed, back to me. "I'd like for you to stay," he admits, and my heart jumps.

"Okay."

He circles the bed and climbs in, and I slide in next to him, and turn off the lamp. He pulls the blankets over me. "Are you warm enough?"

"I am, thanks."

"Okay, we'd better get some sleep. We have an early morning." He kisses my cheek and rolls onto his other side. I lay there for a long moment, willing my heart to slow as my body continues to revel in the way he touched me. After a while, I roll to face him and find his bare back to me. His breathing is slow and steady, and sure that he's asleep, I reach down, grab the blankets and pull on them.

"What are you doing?" he asks, his voice low and groggy.

"Sorry, I thought you were asleep. I'm just covering you up." I tuck the blanket around his shoulder, and he stiffens.

"Jami." His voice takes on a hard edge as he says my name and he moves his shoulders. For a second, I think he's going to shove the blankets off, but the room is cold. I know he runs hot and probably hotter after sex, but his skin was cold to the touch.

"Yes."

A long beat of silence and then, "I...I...it was..." My heart jumps at the pain and thickness in his throat. I've never heard such shame and vulnerability in anyone's voice before. I shift closer and put my arms around him, offering him my comfort and warmth. Whatever it is he wants to tell me, I want him to know I will support and not judge him. "I killed him."

KAI

"Kai," Jami whisper softly and presses a soft kiss to my neck. "I know that isn't true."

How can she say that? She's obviously saying that because that's what the papers said, but they don't know the truth. I'm the only one who does. Although she's probably just consoling me. I'm sure back in the day she never read the papers.

"It's true. Everyone knows it. Why do you think Theo..." Ugh, I hate to even use his name. "...calls me BM."

"I don't know what that means. I wasn't sure I should ask."

"Buddy murderer."

"Ohmigod. I am so sorry, Kai." She tugs on me a bit, urging me to turn and face her and I do.

"You probably want to go back to your room." Look at me pushing her away again, because I know it's for her own good. But if I push her away, will she go back to douche bag? That's certainly not for her own good and I don't want that for her. But I can't forget she has an agenda in this whole bet too.

"No, I don't want to go," she answers quietly. "Unless you really want me to and then I will."

"No," I say shaking my head, but I'm not even sure if I'm doing the right thing. Lately, because of her, I've been thinking with my heart and not my head. "I don't want you to go." Honestly, this is the first time the house feels less empty. She brings a warmth to it, and I like it too much. Fuck.

We both settle on our pillows, our hands touching, our fingers intertwined. She goes very quiet, her eyes moving over my face, in a warm, caring way that pummels my heart until it's nothing but a soft, mushy ball. I am feeling things for this woman, and it's the last thing I want to do. Jesus, nothing good can come from it.

"I'm here if you want to talk," she whispers quietly. "If you don't want to talk and want to just lay here in silence for a while, that's okay too."

With her free hand she pulls my blankets up again after they slip from my shoulders. She keeps her palm on my arm, and while I need the touching to stop—I'm getting in deep here —I need it to continue just as much.

"There was alcohol involved," I begin, pinching my eyes shut as Coop's happy smiling face comes into view.

"You were drinking and driving?" she asks, her brow furrowing, but she keeps her hand on my arm.

"Yes, but no." I pull one hand free and put it on her hip, shifting a little closer.

"I don't understand," she says gently, clearly confused from my confusing answer. "You either were or you weren't."

"There's a fine line, right?" I snort out.

"You were the one driving though?" she straight up asks.

"Yes." I look down, stare at the way my fingers are fisting the blankets at her hip as old memories scrape my insides raw. "We went to a party in his car. He drove, and was supposed to be the designated driver. I thought it was okay to have a couple beers." I shake my head. "I wish I hadn't had any."

Understanding moves into her eyes, and her look is sympathetic as it moves over my face. "I guess Coop didn't keep up his end of the deal, and drank too?"

I swallow as my throat pains. "Yeah, he drank. A lot."

"Why did he do that?"

"His girlfriend broke up with him. Said he'd been drinking too much whenever he went out."

"Was that true?"

"Yeah, I think so. I think it was all the pressure put on him, by our coach, his parents, the fans and media. He was expected to do great things in hockey and I think it was getting to him. I knew things were worrying him, and maybe I should have known better than to trust he wouldn't drink. Then again, maybe he wouldn't have had anything to drink if his girl hadn't broken up with him. Maybe things would have turned out differently."

"That's a lot of maybes, Kai." I fall silent and she continues with, "So at the end of the night, with a couple beers in you, you had to be the driver." I nod. "Were you over the limit?"

"No, but that doesn't matter."

"Did you feel like you were in control? That you didn't drink enough to impair you?"

"Yeah, I mean I thought I was fine, but it was dark and snowing, and..." My stomach squeezes so tight, I'm sure I'm going to vomit. Why am I even telling her all this? What is going on in my life right now? Maybe like Coop, all the pressure is getting to me and I'm ready to snap. I don't know but I do know that it always hurts to think about the accident, which is why I assumed it would hurt to talk about it. While it does hurt, it's also releasing some of the pressure in my chest, pressure that I always carry with me.

"You lost control," she states.

I blink back the tears threatening. "We were following a salt truck. It was spraying the icy roads." I snort out a sad laugh. "I remember thinking, following a salt truck had to be the safest position on an icy road."

"You let down your guard?" she asks, genuine care in her voice.

I give a fast shake of my head. "No, not for a minute." I take a fueling breath. "I'm not sure what happened, but it dumped a huge amount of salt all at once. They think it malfunctioned, but my tire hit the clump, and I lost control. We went over a rail on the highway and a tree..." I stop talking as my throat gurgles, sadness and loss penetrating my bones.

"Kai, I'm so sorry."

"The tree," I try again. "It went through the front window on the passenger side. Coop wasn't supposed to be in the passenger seat. I was...I was the one who was supposed to..."

"No, Kai." Her hand moves to my face, and she cups it gently. "You weren't the one who was supposed to die. Life is crazy, and unpredictable and horrible things happen all the time. Good things happen too, and I truly believe things happen for a reason. Maybe you were right where you were supposed to be, and Coop was where he was supposed to be. Maybe destiny or fate or whatever you want to call it, was playing a hand in everything that happened. You didn't expect Coop to drink, but he did. You didn't expect to be driving, but you did. You didn't expect to go off the road, but you did. Heck, you thought being behind a salt truck was the safest place on the highway."

"It should have been me." I touch the scar above my eye. "This...this is all I walked away with."

She glances at the scar, her eyes sad as she places her hand over my heart. "No, Kai. You walked away with a lot more than that, and you're carrying it all in here."

I exhale as tears push against my half-closed lids. "He...he had so much to offer, Jami." I roll to my back, and put my arm over my forehead as my heart thumps against my chest. I reach for her, and she slides over, and I put my arm around her, and she rests her cheek on my shoulder.

"*You* have a lot to offer, Kai. Don't ever think you don't. You're a great guy, a great hockey player and there are so many people who adore you and cheer for you."

"I don't like that."

"Kai," she says gently. "You have every right to be alive. You did what you thought was the right thing. There was no way you could let Coop drive that night. No way at all. Heck, maybe if you had, you would both have been killed. We don't know that answer, and never will, but you deserve the life you are living, and you deserve to be happy."

"Do you think so?" I ask, wanting it to be true, but feeling guilty about it at the same time.

"Of course, I do." She puts her hand on my stomach, and it feels like an anchor holding me down and stabilizing me. She lifts her head to see me. "Playing hockey, that helps you keep a part of Coop with you."

It's not a question, it's a statement, and I look at her, unable to believe she pieced that together. "Something like that. Is it…stupid?"

"No, Kai, it's not stupid. It's all part of the healing process."

She rolls to her stomach, and braces her chin on her hands as she gazes at me. "His dream was for us to make the NHL together," I tell her.

She angles her head. "His dream? You work your ass off on the ice, and train like mad to fulfill Coop's dream? You avoid relationships because they can distract you from your ultimate goal, all for Coop?"

Wow, way to ask the hard questions. "I mean, I want to do this for him."

"What's *your* dream, Kai?"

"I do want to play in the NHL. In my heart, I do, but it's complicated. I mean, I want to do it for Coop, but I don't feel like I should take any pleasure from it, or that I even deserve it."

"I don't think there is anything wrong with wanting to do it for Coop. I don't. But you need to be doing it for you too. You get one chance at this life, Kai. You truly know that. You can't just be going through the motions and hating yourself when the crowd cheers you on. You deserve the recognition and to be happy."

I swallow, and thread my fingers through hers. "It's just not that easy."

"I don't think Coop's family blames you. I didn't see that when we talked with them. You have to start living your life, because going through the motions isn't what Coop would want."

"No, I don't think he'd want that." I chuckle. "He'd probably kick my ass for it. If the situation were reversed, I know I'd be freaking kicking his ass."

She grins. "Yeah, he probably would. I guess that's why you two were such great friends. You really cared about each other. But it seems you stopped caring about a lot of things so you could focus only on hockey—to fulfill Coop's dream. Maybe it's time to open yourself up again, and do what's right for Kai." I open my mouth to speak, but she continues. "It's scary, I know. But being scared is better than being angry all the time, and alone, don't you think?"

Jesus, she can totally see right through me. I shift to my side again, and my blankets slip. She's about to pull them up again, but I do it first. Our eyes meet, and that's when reality hits me like a fist. I covered myself. I allowed myself comfort. Is Jami right? Do I really deserve a happy life?

"Want to know what I think is good for me right now?" I ask as I move our bodies until she's tucked beneath me.

"Oh, I think I might have an idea," she answers with a grin.

I brush her hair back, the things I'm feeling for this woman scaring me. Is being afraid better than feeling angry? Isn't it the anger that drives me, and if I give in to my feelings, aren't I opening myself up to hurt again? I don't know, but I do know I'm feeling so many things for this incredible woman—things I can't seem to fight off. But I won her in a bet and she's only mine for thirty days. Is it possible that I can convince her to prolong it?

I press my lips to hers and I'm instantly lost in her sweet warmth. "Mmm," she moans and puts her legs around me. My cock thickens against her body, and for the first time in a long time, emotions that aren't hurt build inside me. She lifts her hips, and my cock slips into her warm and welcoming opening.

"Jami," I murmur, and using her heels, she pushes me deeper into her body. I fill her completely, and bury my face in the crook of her neck as we move together. Never in my life has sex been so good. Maybe it's because it was for release only. This time is different, because this time it's with her.

Her hands tighten around my back and I slide mine under her arms and grip her shoulders. The fact that she's so slick and ready for me again blows my mind. I close my eyes and simply feel. Soon enough she's writhing and moaning and scratching at my back and the second her orgasm takes hold, and her muscles clench around me, I give in to the pleasure, accept it in full and climax high inside her.

"Jesus," I cry out as I fully deplete myself within her body, wishing I could have made it last longer because I never want this moment to end. We hold each other tightly as we take gulping breaths. That's when reality hits me. My God, I've never lost myself in anyone like that. Never ever forgotten to put on a condom.

"I'm sorry, Jami." I inch out of her and a hard quiver goes through me. "I didn't use a condom. I don't know what I was thinking."

"You weren't," she tells me with a smile, not at all upset which confuses me. "You were simply feeling and that's not a bad thing."

I roll to my side, and put my hand on her stomach. "Getting pregnant, though. That would be a bad thing."

"I'm protected. I have an implant. Nexplanon." she explains and points to her arm. Then her demeanor changes, and her body tightens. "I know you've been with—"

"Hey, I'm clean," I tell her quickly. "I wouldn't do anything to hurt you, Jami." Does she think I'd purposely hurt her, that I don't care about her well-being. Hell, maybe she does. I wouldn't even so much as call her a friend earlier tonight.

"I wasn't saying that, Kai. It's just...you know."

"Yeah, we all have a reputation, I get it. But I'm clean. I don't have sex without protection." She arches a brow. "Fine. I've never had sex without protection until tonight. I just made a mistake." Oddly enough it didn't feel like a mistake.

Pain and sadness move into her eyes, and I groan. Nothing I'm saying is coming out right. Before I can try again, she says, "I'm clean, too." Her brow crinkles and she looks around, avoiding my gaze. What's going on? Why can't she look at me?

"Jami?" I touch her chin bringing her focus back to me.

A tortured sound climbs out of her throat as she grabs her pillow and puts it over her face. "I don't know how to tell you this. It's kind of embarrassing."

Her words are muffled, so I remove the pillow and take in the way she's nibbling on her bottom lip. "You can tell me."

She throws her arms up and lets them flop at her sides. "I haven't had sex in a while."

I consider that for a second. I'd only just recently won her in a bet and she's been with douche for months. "But...I don't get it."

"I know it's weird." She moans again and rolls to her side. She plucks at imaginary lint. "Somehow I don't...don't think he's attracted to me."

Oh, so we're back to talking about douche bag again. "He's a fucking idiot." Anger surges through me. "You're gorgeous. Any man can see that."

She crinkles up her nose. "I'm not like the girls he usually goes for though, you know."

I nod. I do know, which once again makes me think there's something really off about their relationship. What the hell is that asshole up to? Maybe it's time I found out. Then again, I could just be looking for a reason for them to permanently break up.

Why is that, Kai? Do you want to make Jami yours? Are you really willing to risk your heart?

Maybe I am and maybe my inner thoughts can go fuck themselves.

JAMI

I wake up and slowly open one eye, my body warm and sore in the nicest possible ways. I roll to my side and the second I spot Kai sound asleep beside me, the things we did together last night come rushing back in a whoosh. A smile touches my mouth, and I press my fingers to my kiss-swollen lips. While I like everything about the way last night felt, not to mention this morning, I shouldn't be jumping into bed with Kai, not when this whole thing was to get Theo to realize exactly what he had in me.

What exactly did he have in you, Jami?

Oh, he had a girlfriend who was understanding and kind and supported him twenty-four seven, even leaving him alone after his games so he could party with his friends. Shouldn't I have been invited?

What exactly did you have in him?

Oh, a guy who was popular and loved by all, and never came home with me to help out at the community center. Shouldn't he have been giving me the same support I gave him?

Disliking the dark path my brain is taking, and questioning my life's choices, I push my covers off, and fix them around Kai. All I ever wanted was to feel important, and when the most popular guy on the hockey team paid me attention, it made me feel like I had worth. But I hadn't been feeling that so much, which is why I agreed to go along with the bet when he offered me up to Kai.

I quietly slip from the bed, not wanting to wake Kai when he looks so relaxed and peaceful. I can't deny that last night was pretty spectacular and I'd be lying if I said I didn't want to do it again. I shake my head, so conflicted, as I pull on my clothes.

With the morning light shining in the room, I give it a once over. There are trophies, and medals and an e-reader on his desk. What kind of books does he like? Probably books on how to make him a better hockey player. I don't think I've ever met anyone so obsessed with making it to the NHL and now I know why. Beside the e-reader, I spot a puck shaped dish that holds change and a few lint balls. There are no pictures or memories of Coop at all.

Abandoning his room, I wrap my arms around myself to ward off the early morning chill in the house, and I make my way to the bathroom. I tend to my business and check myself out in the mirror, noticing red blotches on my cheeks. I lean in and realize I'm chaffed from Kai's scruff . Oh, God, will they notice back at Kingston? How will I explain it? Wait, who is even going to ask? Certainly no one at Kingston, but maybe someone from Scotia Academy will, someone like Bree. Again, I don't want to hurt her in any way. She and her friends have been so nice to me and I know how she feels about Kai.

I step from the bathroom and notice the door open in the bedroom down the hall. Coop's old bedroom. I stand still for a second, my gaze going from that bedroom to the one I'd just came from. Would I be doing anything wrong by taking a peek? I'm curious about Kai's best friend, and last night, I learned so much more about Kai and his demons and why he's afraid to get close—to anyone.

I take a step toward Coop's room and stop when the floor creaks. I wait a minute and when Kai doesn't appear, I quietly walk down the hall. I step inside the room, and my heart squeezes in my chest. There's a tote bag on the floor. Was Coop planning to sleep here the night of the accident? I walk around the room, and while this is where Coop slept, I sense Kai everywhere I look.

I run my finger over the old gaming system, and the textbook left abandoned on the desk, still open to an assignment that was probably due the week of the accident. I spot an old phone charger and the e-reader that is way out of date. Was it Kai's or Coop's? My throat tightens, my insides hurting for the man sleeping in the other room when I see the bag of cracker chips half eaten and sealed tight.

"What are you doing in here?"

I jump and spin, shocked at the anger in Kai's voice as he stands in the doorway glaring at me.

"I'm sorry." His hands move to the top of the door frame and his fingers grip it hard. "I didn't mean to pry. I saw the door was open." I hurry toward him. "I'll leave."

He captures my arm, his head dropping as his mood shifts drastically. "I'm sorry, Jami. I'm not mad. Not at you anyway."

Last night, I thought there was a part of him that was going to stop being mad at himself, but it's clear that's not going to happen overnight, not when he's been carrying so much blame around for so long.

"I'm sorry," I tell him again. "I shouldn't have come in here."

"Maybe it's time someone did," he says quietly, and steps into the room, glancing at the textbook on the desk. He stares at the book for so long, I start to shift back and forth, not sure whether to walk away or walk closer. He finally speaks. "We had an assignment due." He takes small steps to the desk, and lightly runs his fingers over the book. A chuckle that holds fond memories fills the space between us. "Coop never was good at math. I used to help him."

"You were a good friend," I murmur softly and quietly, not wanting to interrupt his happier thoughts.

His head lifts and his gaze zeros in on me. "I'm sorry, Jami. Last night, when I was talking to the Coopers, I..."

"It's okay."

"No, it's not okay. You are my friend."

I smile and step up to him. "You're my friend too, Kai."

He nods, and his body goes still when he glances over my shoulder and sees the duffle bag on the floor. "It's been a long time since I've been in this room." He bends and kisses my forehead, filling my heart in strange ways, before stepping around me. My throat grows so tight it hurts as he stands over the duffle bag that clearly holds a lot of memories for him.

"Do you think we should look in it?" I ask. Maybe it will bring back more happy memories for him.

"I know what's in it," he answers almost absentmindedly.

"Is that your bag?" I walk over to the neatly made bed but don't sit.

"No, it's Coop's."

"What's in it?" I ask, giving him an opportunity to talk about it if he wants.

"Books, probably his football hoodie, sweats, pajama pants."

"It was his overnight bag?"

"He kept a lot of clothes here, but he always carried stuff with him." He chuckles again. "You know, he was big and tough, but he hated being cold."

"Really."

"I don't know what it was about him, but he didn't even like swimming in the ocean because the water was too cold."

"The ocean is cold."

A smile touches his mouth. "He was just a funny guy. Lots of quirks, but that's what made him even more loveable." A pause and then, "Everyone really loved him."

"He sounds pretty amazing."

He crouches to toys with the zipper, but there's a new kind of calmness as he reminisces. "There's this bridge, you know, the one in Wolfville that everyone jumps off."

I nod as I take in the gleam in his eyes. "I know it."

"Have you done it? Jumped off it, I mean."

I laugh. "Do you think my parents would have let me do that? I was bubble wrapped, remember?"

"Yeah, I know." He nudges me. "But I don't think that would have stopped you. I mean, you climbed that tree when you weren't supposed to."

"I suppose I did, but no. I've never jumped. Was it fun?"

He picks the bag up, sits on the bed and sets it on his lap. I stand there, not sure what to do, until he pats the spot beside him and I sit down. "It was. For everyone except Coop." He laughs. "I can't tell you how many times he'd stand on the edge and then chicken out."

"So, he didn't like heights, and he didn't like to be cold."

"That bridge combined those two things," he says with a laugh. "He also hated rain, but loved rainbows."

"You know what they say, the brightest rainbows follow the darkest rainstorms." He frowns like that's giving him a lot to think about, and I ask, "Did he ever eventually jump?"

"Actually yeah, it was the summer before..."

"Before the accident," I say, finishing his sentence for him and using the word accident on purpose, because that's exactly what it was. Kai might have been driving but he was not responsible for Coop's death.

"I have a video."

"No way, can I see?"

He sets the bag down, and jumps up. "Hang on." I sit quietly, my heart pounding as he darts from the room and comes back with his phone. He sits back down beside me, and scrolls through his videos until he finds it. His finger hovers over the play button for a second and I suspect it's been a long time since he's watched it.

"I bet he loved it after he did it."

He laughs. "I'll take that bet."

"You take a lot of bets," I mutter with a grin, and lean into him. He just shakes his head and presses play and I move closer as we watch Coop stand at the bridge as his friends cheer him on. They're all joking and laughing and Coop is telling everyone to fuck off, which is really funny.

"Come on, Coop, you got this," I hear Kai urge as he records.

"How many times did you record before he finally did it?"

"You don't even want to know. But I did it every time just in case."

"Good thing."

From the video Coop asks, "You'll still give me your Crosby card?"

"You know it," Kai responds and when I arch a brow, he explains that it's a hockey trading card.

"Here goes nothing, you fuckers!" Coop belts out and pushes off the rail. He lands with an undignified splash and curses how cold the water is after he resurfaces. His friends laugh and congratulate him as he swims to the embankment.

I clap my hands. "Did you give him the card?"

He gives me a look that suggests I should never have questioned that. "Hey, I'm a guy who follows through with his bets."

I rub his arm and give him a peck on the cheek. "Yeah, I know you do." He sets his phone down and grabs the bag. "Do you think the card is in there?" He nods. "Should we open it?"

A hiss fills the air as he slides the zipper open. The first thing he pulls out is a hoodie with their high school crest. The next is sweatpants, and then a very sticky piece of gum, oozing from the wrapper.

I inch back. "What the heck?"

Kai bursts out laughing. "How the hell did I forget this?" he asks holding up the disgusting piece of gum that at one time might have been rectangular-shaped. He laughs as he holds it out for me to see. "Want some?"

I push his hand away. "Eww."

"He was so superstitious," he explains, grabbing a tissue from the box on the nightstand. "He chewed gum before every game and had to spit it out just before we left the locker room."

"Ugh." He sets the gum on the nightstand to dispose of later.

"That gum brand is good, though. Did you chew it too?"

He laughs. "Like he would share it."

I put my hand on his back and rub gently. "Do you have any superstitions?"

"Nope," he jokes and adds. "But if I did and it involved baby powder, I certainly wouldn't tell you." As I laugh, he pulls out the Crosby card. He gives a slow shake of his head as he turns it over in his hand. "He never really intended to keep it."

"He was just messing with you, carrying it around to taunt you," I say with a laugh and then sneeze horribly. My eyes begin to water, and he grabs a tissue and hands it to me.

"Still Allergic huh?"

"Apparently."

"Maybe you're not," he teases with a tilt of his head. "Maybe you're just trying to get me naked again."

"Or...maybe I'm trying to get you to get me naked," I tease. He chuckles and looks at the card. "So, he liked to taunt you with it, huh?"

"That was Coop."

He shifts on the bed, turning to me, a small smile on his lips. I touch his cheek and can almost feel the pain shifting, a new, albeit fragile, sense of peace and acceptance about him. "I wish you could have met him."

I put my hand on his heart. "You keep him so close, I feel like I know him."

"He would have liked you."

My heart thumps at the warmth in his gaze as it moves over my face. "Even though I'm the enemy?" I chuckle. "Although now that I know what you do to your enemies..."

"Are you talking about last night?" he asks a wry grin on his face.

"Yes, I am, and if that's what you do with your enemies, maybe I never want to be your friend."

Keeping the card, he leaves the bag on the bed and stands. He tucks the card into the edge of the mirror near the closet and turns to me, holding out his hands. "We'd better get to the vineyard before I'm tempted to take you back to my bed."

Not that I'm opposed, but I know he wants to help out today, so I stand and slide my hand into his. I head toward the door, but stop when he gives my hand a tug.

"Hey," he whispers.

I stop and turn and the second I do, his head dips and his lips close over mine for a deep, mind-numbing kiss that wraps around my body and my heart. He holds me to him for a long time, and it's almost like I can feel the grief ease from his body. He finally breaks the kiss and smiles at me as he tucks my hair behind my ear.

"What was that for?" I ask, totally aroused and breathless.

"For this..." he says and glances at the room behind us.

"Hey," I say, shrugging like it's nothing, even though it's something and I'm so damn happy I could be there for him. I just wish I could have been there for him years ago. To think how much pain he's been in all this time breaks my heart. "What are friends for?" I say.

He leans in and lightly brushes my lips. "I think you mean girlfriend."

What the heck? Did he just seriously call me his girlfriend—without sarcasm?

KAI

I take her hand, a new lightness in my step as we head downstairs. Since we're running late, I hurry my steps, wanting to catch my parents before they head out to the vineyard. Chatter from the kitchen reaches our ears, and the back door creaks open. The last time I brought a girl home was...never. But Mom and Dad are going to love Jami.

Love.

What a strange word and it's definitely not something I feel for her. I can't because I only have her for one month, right? We step into the kitchen and Mom and Dad both stop at the doorway, and turn our way. They're dressed in overalls and sunhats, ready to work the day away.

"Kai," Mom calls and hurries over to give me a hug. "We heard you were here. We looked for you last night, but you disappeared." She turns to Jami and grins. "And I can see why."

"Way to be subtle, Mom," I joke and Jami shifts beside me. "Mom, Dad, this is Jami. She's from Greenwood and goes to Kingston College in the city."

They both look surprised for a moment, but Dad shakes it off first. "It's so nice to meet you, Jami."

"Nice to meet you too, Mr. Ward."

"Mr. Ward is my dad. You call me Bill."

"And I'm Marie," Mom says. "You both look like you need coffee."

"Gee, why don't you tell me what you really think," I tease, and Mom cups my cheeks and laughs. Her eyes narrow as they move over my face, checking in on me like she usually does, and this time, I don't squirm under her scrutiny. "You look good, Kai."

"I'm good, Mom." Her eyes narrow more and that's when I realize that's what I always say whether I truly am good or not. It's a knee jerk reaction. I just hate when they worry about me, and they worry about me a lot. That's what parents do. Maybe it's good for Jami to see this.

"You're eating well?" she asks, as she steps away and grabs two mugs from the cupboard.

"Jami's brother is a chef and her mom makes a mean lasagna. All we've been doing is eating."

"Are you guys here for the day?" Dad asks, looking a bit conflicted, because he knows he's needed in the vineyard, but doesn't want to miss out on family time with me.

"Yes, we're going to help out with the grapes."

"Oh honey, no. You don't have to do that. You have enough on your plate with school and hockey, and..." Mom blinks at Jami. "Your new friend."

"Jami is interested in learning, and you know I love it in the vineyard."

"I know, Kai, but we have lots of hands helping today. Maybe you guys could go for a nice relaxing hike."

"I really want to help," Jami pipes in.

"Well then, it's settled," Dad says. "Another set of hands always comes in handy."

"I don't know how much help I'll be." Jami blinks nervously. "I've never done it before. I don't want to ruin any of the grapes. But I am really interested."

"You won't ruin anything, because I'll teach you everything you need to know," I tell her, and put my arm around her to pull her close. She smiles up at me, no doubt surprised by the public display of affection, and I love when she looks at me like that. I love a lot of things, actually. Maybe too many things. "I have faith in you."

"Why don't you guys start in the west field? Jackson is coming by to do a big barbecue for everyone at noon."

I nod. "Okay, we'll see you both at noon."

They head out the door, and I step up to the coffee pot and pour two mugs. "Jackson?" she asks.

"Oh, Jackson is Dad's brother. He likes to help during the harvest by cooking for all the workers. He's super funny, you're going to love him."

"Can't wait to meet him. You're surrounded by great people, Kai. Including your friends back at Scotia Academy."

"Yeah," is all I say. She's right and maybe I haven't been treating them fairly, not even recognizing them as *friends*. I grab the milk from the fridge and pour it into our mugs as she glances at her yoga pants and sweater.

She plucks at her sweater and twists her lips. "I'm not sure I'm dressed for this."

I eye her for a second, admiring her every lush curve. I moan in appreciation and say, "I actually think you're overdressed."

She arches her brow, clearly confused. "This is overdressed for the vineyard?"

"No, for the bedroom." She sneezes again. "Wow, your allergies really are bad." I frown. "Do you think you should sit out the harvest?"

"No way. I'm looking forward to learning and seeing how and where you guys make all the wine. How many chances does a girl from Greenwood get a behind the scenes look at her rival's operation?"

"Wait, are you planning to sabotage things in the vineyard? Sneak in like a Trojan horse and take out the enemy? Is that your real agenda?" I ask, and it suddenly brings a knot to my stomach because it reminds me of her agenda: to make her boyfriend jealous so he appreciates her more. Has anything about that changed since last night? Am I a fool to believe sex might have brought us closer together? Jesus, what is even happening to me?

"You're the one who invited me, the enemy, into your territory, Kai," she teases, totally unaware of the storm inside me.

"True, so basically what you're saying is, if anything bad happens it would, ultimately, be my fault." Christ, I feel that. I feel that so hard. If I fell for her and something bad happened, it would totally be my fault. Truthfully, after being angry for so long, I know I'm starting to feel other things again, but there's a small part of my brain that's sending out warning signals reminding me it's far too dangerous to open myself up to loss and pain again.

"Kai, everything that happens is not your fault." She throws her hands up in the air. "And since I'm not Helen of Troy, nobody from Greenwood will be sending over huge wooden horses. We're two consenting adults, and whatever happens between us, is our joint responsibility. Okay?"

"Okay," I respond, a little amused at her outburst.

"Now, I really like your parents," she says, changing the subject as her gaze strays to the door.

"They'd keep me in a bubble, too if they could. You saw with your own eyes and heard how overprotective my mother is."

"It's probably because you've been through hell, and maybe she knows how easy it could have been to lose you in that accident too."

I pull her to me and while I don't want to upset her, I'm not sure she saw what I did when her mother looked at her. Pure love and motherly concern. "Parents worry, Jami. When they're good at parenting, it's their one and only job. After the accident, mine knew what I've gone through and they've gone through a lot too. They don't want anything to happened to me because they love me. Just like yours want to keep you in bubble wrap, too. It's because they care about you." I lightly poke her chest. "*You*, this great daughter who they're so very proud of. Not the child who was born to help save her brother, and while that might be the case, and I'm not denying it. They love you, Jami."

She glances down, and steps into me. "I was so sheltered, I guess I didn't realize all parents were like mine."

"I'm not sure they all are, but when there is tragedy in the family, it can definitely change the dynamics. When you become a parent, you'll see."

"Who says I'm becoming a parent?" she asks.

"What, are you kidding me? I saw you with those kids. You'll be a great mom."

She shrugs. "Do you want kids?"

"I don't know," I say honestly, my stomach clenching. "I don't know what I want, other than making the NHL."

"Wanting anything else, and not being able to get it, or worse, get it and lose it, is scary, right?" she asks, understanding me so damn well.

"Yeah." I pick up my coffee cup and take a much-needed sip.

As if sensing I don't want to talk about what really scares me, she says, "You know, I think I'll shoot Mom a text and let her know we'll stop by on our way home today."

"I think she'd love that."

Love...there's that word again. I inch back and take a sip of coffee and work to pull myself together, because I'm suddenly bombarded with so many different emotions. As she sends off a text, I clear my throat and say, "We have some spare coveralls and hats in the barn. We should get at it before it gets too hot."

She smiles as a text from her mom instantly comes back. My heart hurts to think she believes she has no real value, or isn't important. It's so not the case.

"You mean the barn Cotton escapes from?" she asks, a new lightness about her.

"Yes, I'm sure she's out wandering and scaring the crap out of the workers." I grab a freshly baked muffin from the tray and hold it out to her. "I can make eggs," I tell her.

"This is plenty."

We scarf down muffins, finish our coffee and head out into the bright sunshine. Her phone pings as we follow the path to the barn, and she pulls it from her pocket. I glance at her as she sends a quick message and I want to ask if it's douche bag, but don't want to come off as possessive. "My mom," she tells me with a chuckle. "Checking to make sure I'm dressed properly for today's sun."

I nod and relax a bit. "Your mom is the best."

"Yeah," is all she says we walk toward the barn in silence, both of us lost in our own thoughts. The door creaks as I open the empty barn, the animals are all out for the day. I pull two pairs of coveralls off the hook and drop a big floppy hat on her head. "This should make your mom happy." She looks so damn adorable all I want to do is take her up to the loft and make love to her.

Make love to her?

What the hell? When did I become a Hallmark movie?

I grab two big buckets and two sets of pruning shears. She has an aura of excitement about her as we leave the barn and head to the west vineyard. We walk by some of the workers, and I say hello, recognizing them from previous years.

"It smells so good here," she says and inhales.

"A lot better than jet fuel, huh?" I joke making a jab at living on an air force base.

"You're actually right about that."

"Score one for Middleton." I raise my hand in victory.

"So, we are keeping score, are we?" she asks. I just grin at her and when we reach the orchard where my folks asked us to work, I take the shears from the bucket and hand them to Jami. She glances around, eagerness about her. "What do I do?"

I smile at her, absolutely loving the sense of adventure in her. It's not something I've had in a long time, and her enthusiasm is rubbing off on me.

"It's so easy. Just hold the grapes like this and cut close to the stalk." I pluck a couple of grapes from the cluster before I gently set them in the bucket. I hold one juicy purple grape out. "Open." She does and I drop the grape onto her tongue.

She bites into it and instead of expressing joy, she winces. "Ohmigod, Kai, that is so sour." Her nose crinkles as she forces herself to swallow.

"You don't like that?"

She shakes her head and her hat flops around. "No, what was it?"

"It's a Foch."

"Why is it so sour?"

I laugh and pop one into my mouth. "They're actually my favorite."

"What is wrong with your taste buds?" she asks and wipes her mouth with the back of her hand.

"There isn't a thing wrong with my taste buds," I tell her and put my arm around her waist, dragging her closer to me I press my lips to hers, and slide my tongue in, tasting the sweet grape juice in her mouth. I press against her and she drops her shears and puts her arms around my back. The warmth of the sun beats down on us as we hold onto one another, and when I break the kiss, her eyes are glossy. "I know sweet when I taste it," I tell her as I brush my tongue over my bottom lip.

"I know sour when I taste it, but you know what, when I taste the grapes like this, they actually tastes pretty good."

"I'll grab us a bottle of wine from the store. It's a medium, full-bodied red with distinctive berry flavors."

"I wonder if my brother carries your wines at his restaurant. If not, he should be."

"Speaking of restaurants. Can you guess what this pairs well with?"

"Hmm, let me guess," she teases as she looks up, thinking about it. "Lamb or beef?"

"Cheezies and ketchup potato chips," I tell her and she laughs. "Oh, and an action flick, of course. We can try it later tonight, back in the city." She frowns like she's not sure of that. "Unless you have plans?"

"Actually, I kind of do."

"Oh, no problem," I say and let it go. If she doesn't want to tell me that's not a problem.

She hesitates, like she doesn't want to carry on with this conversation, but then, she must change her mind because she says, "I have curling practice tonight."

"Great, I'll go with you and then we'll make dinner and have some wine."

Her hand lands on my arm. "You really don't have to, Kai. I know it's boring."

"I doubt it, and I'm your boyfriend. Supporting you is part of the package."

Her brow bunches together. "Kai, you don't have to."

I love that she has my best interests at heart here, but she's wrong, thinking I'll be bored. "I want to," I tell her firmly, so she closes her mouth. That's when it hits me. I could very well be overstepping, wanting more than she's willing to give in this relationship. "Unless you don't want me there?

Her smile is soft and sweet. "I think it would be nice to have you there."

"Settled." I gesture toward the vine. "Now show me how it's done." She holds the cluster gently and snips the vine. She holds it out to me, completely proud of herself. "Well done."

We both turn to the vines and we talk about school, and homework, and her brother's Halloween party as we work. At times we fall silent, and it's completely natural and comfortable, just the two of us enjoying each other's company. Voices sound in the distance as everyone works, and birds chirp overhead, wanting to get in on the action.

"I can see why you like it out here," she says quietly. "You're going to miss this when you go off to play in the NHL."

"I will, but maybe someday I'll have my own vineyard. You know, the greatest hockey player of all time has his own winery in Ontario."

"Niagara-on-the-Lake. I've always wanted to visit the region. I hear it's gorgeous. There's no reason why you can't follow in his footsteps after hockey."

I grin, liking that idea and for the first time in a long time, I start to think of a life outside of the rink. "He even has a restaurant."

"Maybe by then, my brother will have more than one, and can open one on your estate."

I laugh. "Way to keep it in the family. And what will you be doing on this estate?" I ask jokingly. As soon as the words leave my mouth, I regret them. Talking like we have a future will only scare her off, right? I'm about to somehow try and grab my stupid words back, and stuff them to the bottom of my throat, when she grins and plays along.

"Oh, I don't know. Picking grapes in the sun and drinking wine sounds just about right. Wait, is there going to be a pool? If there's going to be a pool, I change my answer."

"Okay, yes, there's going to be a pool," I say loving the dreamy look on her face. "How does that change things?"

"Because if there's a pool, I'll be lounging and swimming, and there will probably be some wine involved. Maybe not this Foch stuff."

"I think you'll like it once you try it."

"There's a lot of things I like once I've tried it," she murmurs, and I can't help but grin. We go back to working and cutting grapes.

I can't help but ask, "Will you be in a bikini at the pool?" My gaze moves over her body as she reaches above her head. She's in coveralls and there's nothing sexy about that, but somehow on her, everything works.

"Of course not. If it's my own private pool, I'll probably go naked."

"Jesus, Jami," I groan, and shift my cock in my pants. She notices and seems quite pleased with herself. I give myself a moment to picture this fantasy that in no way can ever happen. I like it. A lot. But it's just a fantasy, right? I don't deserve a beautiful life like that. Or do I?

JAMI

I honestly can't believe one full week has passed since the bet and I've pretty much spent every spare moment with Kai at the hockey rink, the curling rink and my place. We don't go to his. I know his roommate Thomas; we grew up together and he's a total man whore. Not that there's anything wrong with that. He's single, and can be with whoever he wants, but we want our privacy so we stay at my place.

Honestly, I had so much fun picking grapes at his vineyard and getting to meet his family and hanging out and laughing with the farm workers as his uncle fed us hamburgers and hotdogs. I guess my favorite part of all this is simply how easy he is to be with, how he encourages and supports me, even going to my curling practice and watching a game last week.

Curling certainly isn't as exciting as the game playing out on the ice before me, especially considering it's against Kingston, and Kai and Theo look like they're about to get into a fight every five minutes. Wait, does that mean Theo would fight for me? That thought makes me laugh. Just a couple of weeks ago he was happy to hand me over to his enemy.

"Something funny?" Bree asks from beside me, and I turn to her. I really like Bree. She's so sweet and supportive of Kai, and all her friends, and every time she looks at me with those big vulnerable doe eyes, my heart hurts a little. It's easy to tell how much she likes Kai, and I swore I would never come between them.

I'm such a horrible person.

"Oh, I was just remembering something from a while ago," I fib, and she nods.

She turns back to the ice, and as I take in her profile, she says, "Looks like your boyfriend just got a penalty."

"Really?" I search for Kai, only to realize she's talking about Theo. My stomach clenches. I guess in her mind and everyone else's, Theo is still my boyfriend. Why wouldn't she think that? From that very first night, Kai made it perfectly clear that this was just about a bet. Everyone would naturally assume it was to put Theo in his place plus he told everyone to be nice to me. And they have all been nice and inclusive, bringing me into their circle, but do I really belong? Are they all just pretending to be my friends?

When this is over, when I'm no longer useful, will they simply cast me aside, making me feel like I was nothing but a means to an end...the way I've felt my whole life? But Kai told me I had value, and that's why he bet on me.

Did he mean that, or was he just trying to make me feel better? Honestly, I have to lean toward the former, because the man treats me with such respect and makes me feel like the most important person in the world to him. My heart soars as I briefly close my eyes, my body remembering the way he always touches me with such care and tenderness.

When I open my eyes again, I see Theo's hard face, and notice the way he's glaring at me. I can almost feel his anger, but what right does he have to be angry? He agreed to the bet, and really when it comes down to it, we're broken up, so he has no say in what I do. I'm not even sure I'm that same desperate girl I was just a week ago. Desperate to be seen for who I am, for someone to love me. God, how pathetic was I?

Summer, who is Bree's roommate, sits on the other side of Bree. I love how close they are, although it also hurts, considering the way my roommate has nothing to do with me. Summer leans over and puts her hand on my leg. "Girl, that man looks like he's going to eat you alive. When you guys get back together, he is going to rock your world," she says with a laugh as she playfully puts her hands over her ears. "I don't want to be within fifty miles of your place when he comes knocking."

"Yeah," is all I respond with and steal a fast glance at Bree, who is nibbling on her bottom lip. She almost looks like she's going to cry and my heart sinks into my stomach. She must know what's going on between Kai and me. She must know I've developed feelings for the man.

"Absence makes the heart grow fonder," Summer adds with a snap of her fingers and her gum.

"That was the plan," I murmur. It might have started out that way, but maybe that isn't what's really going on here. Maybe Theo just wants what he can't have and my plan, which was a stupid one to begin with, won't change anything long term for him. If we get back together, maybe he'll fall back to his old ways. My God, we were a couple. Neither one of us were seeing anyone else and had no plans to, but he wouldn't even admit to Kai that we were exclusive.

"Kai is seriously enjoying rubbing his win in Theo's face," Summer notes. "You guys have been spending every minute together."

"Yeah." I swallow as Bree shifts uncomfortably beside me.

"Winning looks good on Kai," she adds. "He seems…"

"Happy," Bree says, and gives me a wobbly smile.

"Yeah, just a little bit more mellow, and not as angry or intense anymore," Summer adds, her gaze going back to Theo as he stews in the penalty box. "You two are getting back together, right?"

"What?" I ask, surprised by the question.

"I just mean, if you're not." She winks. "He is kind of hot."

Bree nudges Summer. "Stop."

"What? He's hot." She throws her arms up and laughs. "It's just an observation and I'm sure Jami doesn't mind me looking. How lucky are you anyway, Jami?" She nudges Bree, who falls into me. "Hanging with the two hottest guys in the city."

"Yeah, lucky me," I say. Needing to change the topic, I ask, "Did you get a costume for tomorrow night's Halloween party?"

"I am so looking forward to it," Summer says and snaps her gum. "I'm going as a sexy cop." She wags her eyebrows suggestively, and I love the confidence she has. "I plan to make lots of arrests."

I smile as I envision her in her outfit, which I know she'll rock. "Bree, what about you?"

"Cave girl. I actually made the costume."

"I can't wait to see it." I remember her mentioning she was in design. "I don't have that kind of talent."

"What are you going as?" she asks, her big eyes wide and curious. "Is Kai dressing up?"

I nod. "When Kai and I were in the valley," I begin and notice the tightness in her body. "Well, we stopped at the big Halloween store there, and we're going as Betty and Jughead from Riverdale. We thought that would be fun seeing as the party is at my brother's restaurant, and we can pretend it's Pop's Diner."

"Girl," Summer says. "Did you miss the memo?"

"Memo?" I ask. Oh, God what did I miss?

She leans across Bree, all conspiratorial like. "Halloween is the perfect time to dress sexy. You should have at least gone as Veronica."

"Oh, I didn't…"

Bree puts her hand on mine. "I think it's a cute idea, and if you want to spice Betty up, come by our place. I can help you."

God, she is so sweet and I am such a horrible person.

"Actually, come by anyway," Summer says. "I meant to tell you, a bunch of us are getting together to pre-drink and we want you there. It should be fun. Six good? Your brother wants us there for eight, right?"

My heart thumps. They want me there. That is so nice, and while I've always wanted my own special group of friends, after sleeping with Kai—knowing how Bree feels—I'm not sure I deserve their kindness.

As Bree watches me for a reaction, I answer quietly, "I'd like that."

The crowd goes crazy and I turn my focus back to the rink, just as Kai catches the puck on his blade and takes a shot. Theo jumps the boards, his penalty over, but he's too late to stop the goal. We all jump to our feet and I don't miss the way Kai's eyes stray to me, a smile on his face.

Summer gasps. "Ohmigod, look at him staring at you. Like he hasn't pissed Theo off enough." Theo starts toward him, but his teammates stop him and I'm happy about that. I don't want anything messing with Kai's chances for the NHL. That's when I see his coach talking to some man, and I wonder if it's a scout. Kai said there would be some here tonight. I really want that to happen for him for so many reasons.

My phone pings and I pull it from my pocket. I expect it to be my mother checking in on me. She hasn't said much about Kai. We stopped in to see them on the way home from the valley and Dad really seemed to like Kai. I'm surprised to see that it's my brother checking in with me again, wanting to make sure Brad still plans on attending the party. I grin, having met Brad a few times, I really think the two of them would be awesome together.

By the time I text back and put my phone away, the game is over, and I jump to my feet and start cheering. Theo glares at me as he skates toward center ice, and he points toward the doors, like he wants me to meet him. Should I? He hasn't texted me, not since Kai took my phone and told him to back the fuck off, because if he didn't, Kai would break the rules too. Lord, is that what is going on here? Is he showing me how a woman should be treated. Is that why I'm falling for Kai? Wait, am I falling for him? I am, God, I really am. Maybe I should meet with Theo and tell him that.

"Looks like Romeo wants you back," Summer says.

"Yeah." I don't look at him, instead I follow them from the stands and we head outside, to where the Scotia players come out. I shift from one foot to the other, debating on telling Kai about Theo's message, but decide against it. I don't want them getting into a fight, especially not when scouts are here.

Chatter is loud as we all wait, and soon enough the players start filing out. I search for Kai, and my stomach tightens when he's nowhere to be found. I naturally think the worst, that he and Theo are in some locker room fighting it out.

Lots of the girls jump on the backs of the players and get piggyback rides to the pub for beer and nachos. That's when I notice Bree on Brennan's back and it's easy to tell he likes her. I take my phone from my pocket to text Kai when he comes bursting out the door.

A huge smile lights up his face when he finds me standing there. "Kai?" I ask.

He hurries to me, picks me up and spins me around. "Babe," he begins, and before he can finish the sentence, his lips find mine for a deep, sensual kiss and my body relaxes into him. He moans into my mouth and I wrap my arms around him. He finally inches back and I grip his coat—it might not be zipped up but at least he's finally wearing one—and can't help but smile. He's so happy, and I love everything about this.

"What is going on?"

"I was just invited to an evaluation camp."

"Kai!" I yell. "That is amazing." I cup his cheeks and kiss him again. "I am so proud of you." I spot movement behind us, but when I look into the shadows, I don't see anything. "When do you go."

"Next weekend."

"That soon?"

"Yes, and I'm going to miss you, so tonight after the pub, I'm going to take you back to my place and show you how much."

I laugh, loving his enthusiasm. "Wait, which team?"

"Edmonton."

My heart floats in my chest. "That's the team you wanted." I kiss him again, unable to get enough. "We're definitely celebrating, but I think I'm going to take you back to your place and show *you*..." I poke him in the chest. "How much I'll miss you."

"Well, if you insist," he says with a laugh, and puts his arm around me.

"Also, you smell extra baby-powdery tonight," I tease.

He grins, never having admitted to using baby powder or where that superstition started. We start toward the pub, and he says, "It was the gum."

He pulls a package of gum from his pocket. After we returned from our trip to the valley, the first thing I did was buy him Coop's brand of gum to help him keep Coop close and his best friend's tradition alive. He loved it, and took me to bed to show me just how much.

"It was definitely the gum," I agree. "And Coop cheering you on. He would be so proud of you, Kai."

"Yeah," he says his voice filled with warmth and love as his arm tightens around my shoulder. As we walk beneath a streetlight, I take in his handsome profile, and as if sensing me watching, he turns to me. "How about we skip the pub and go straight to my place?"

"While I would like that, you need to be there. I don't want any of your friends hating me for keeping you from your after-game party." Heck, I know one who probably already hates me big time. He looks like he's about to protest, so I say again, "You need to be there, and we all have something huge to celebrate."

He stops and pulls me to him, pushing his beautiful thickening cock against my sex, letting me know how much he wants me. "But babe, I need to be in here."

I laugh as my body warms, wanting nothing more than his cock inside me. "Speaking of something huge..."

KAI

As my buddies and I walk toward Kellan's new restaurant, I can't seem to wipe the smile from my face. Next weekend, I'm going to evaluation camp, and hopefully my dreams—and Coop's dreams—will come true.

I glance around at my friends—yes, they're my friends—and the mood is light and happy tonight, especially after our winning streak lately. At first I found it odd that Jami said she'd meet me here, but then when I found out she was getting ready with Bree, Summer and a few of their friends, it flooded me with happiness.

I'm so happy to see how well they've bonded, and it's clear, after spending so much time with Jami, that she lacks any real female friendships at Kingston. Hell, I met her roommate, and while she seemed nice, there was no bond between her and Jami, and that really sucks. If only Jami could move in with someone from Scotia Academy. But that's a ridiculous thought. We're rival schools, but nothing about Jami and I are in opposition. In fact, we fit together perfectly.

"What are you grinning about, Jughead?" Brennan asks me.

"Nothing." I shove him playfully, and he trips on his cape, nearly doing a face plant.

"Dude," he yells at me and I help keep him upright.

"Sorry," I apologize and try to hide my smile. I can't believe Jami talked me into being Jughead, but she seemed so excited by the idea. Or was it me who was excited by it? I have no idea who I'm becoming around her, but I don't hate it.

We reach the restaurant and I pull the door open. Brad, dressed as a game of Twister, pushes ahead of us and steps inside, his gaze searching the restaurant. I shake my head at his anxious antics, but I also think he and Kellan will be a good team. Just like Jami and I are a good team.

Suddenly the hairs on my nape rise and after everyone enters, I turn and glance down the dark street, searching for movement under the streetlights. Do we have a straggler amongst us?

I wait a second and when no one appears, I enter the restaurant to find it decorated with carved pumpkins, black streamers, and propped skeletons dressed as servers. Delicious smells come from the kitchen, and I inhale, looking to see if Jami and the others have arrived yet. When my gaze comes up empty, disappointment settles in my gut.

"Kai!" Kellan yells out as he weaves his way through the crowd towards me. "Where's Jami?" he asks, and then stands back to take in my outfit. "Aren't you the cutest."

"Yeah, the cutest. Just what I always wanted."

He laughs and puts his hand on my arm. "Does she have you whipped already?"

"What?"

"Oh, come on." He waves his hand up and down the length of my ridiculous costume, and I scrub my head, moving the itchy hat around. "Methinks there is only one set of big blue eyes that could have talked you into this." I shake my head again, in defeat this time, and he leans into me. "For what it's worth, I think you two are cute together."

"Yeah?" I ask, clinging to that like dryer lint because I'm that pathetic, but I like that he's letting me know I'm welcomed into his family. I'm used to people pushing me away, or me pushing them away after the accident, assuming everyone hated me and knowing I deserved it.

Maybe I don't deserve the hatred, but does that mean I'll fully open myself up to love and hurt again? Yeah, I think I might be, slowly, inch by inch, because Jami is worth it.

But what if you hurt her, dude?

"Between you and me, I never liked Theo," Kellan adds. "I might be the only one."

My hackles rise as Kellan voices Theo's name. "Nope, you're not. Theo and I go way back." I glance around the room at everyone having fun. "What do you really know about him?"

"Not much." Kellan shrugs. "We grew up in the same community, and everyone loved him, still do. But the person who loves Theo the most is Theo. He thinks he's God's gift to the universe and especially to women."

"Did he come from a good family?"

"A really good family. His father is the base commander, and they don't get higher up than that. He's strict and has high expectations of Theo. He was never allowed to step out of line...although that one time..."

He lets his voice fall off. "What?" My heart jumps, sensing there is more to Theo than we all know.

"Well." He leans into me, even though the volume in the restaurant is high as everyone is hanging out and eating the snacks being carried around by the servers. "He was smoking behind the resource center. Flicked a cigarette into the garbage can and it set on fire. It spread and damn near burned the center down." He gives a low slow whistle. "We actually didn't see him for weeks after that. I figured his father had sent him to military school or something. But I guess he didn't because he's so good at hockey. Hell, he didn't even get into trouble with the town, because..." he rolls his eyes. "Hockey." Then as if realizing what he said, he apologizes. "Sorry, I didn't mean to insult you. I'm not saying—"

"No, I get it. Exceptions are made for good players."

Is he thinking an exception was made for me after Coop died? He's older than Jami, probably heard all about it. As if reading my mind, his face goes serious. "I understand what happened with you and your friend was an accident, Kai. I didn't know you back then, but I do now, and I want to say I'm so sorry for your loss."

His sincerity warms me. "Thank you." I put my hands in my pant pockets and sort of rock back and forth on my feet, not used to condolences from people, especially those from our rival town. But Jami is right, and it's time we moved past that.

He smoothes his hands down his perfectly tailored white chef's coat. "You know, I always thought Jami and Theo were a strange couple."

I cock my head and study his concerned expression. "Why do you say that?"

"Theo sort of let loose when he got out from beneath his father's thumb, although I still think his father has a lot of control, but he's not here, in the city, to oversee Theo's every movement."

My breathing quickens. "Let loose how?"

"Back home he dated nice girls. Like straight A students. Good girls, who follow the rules and will put him on a pedestal. I'm not saying the women I've seen him with here, before Jami, haven't been nice, and women can sleep with whoever they want, there's nothing wrong with that. It's just not Jami's style. I think she's more the long term, marrying kind of girl, you know."

"I do know," I answer as that knot in my stomach tightens, confirming my theory that there is something off about their relationship and Theo might be up to something. But what only Kellan and I might know is that Jami has a rebellious side, one she keeps hidden. But I'm sure Theo has no idea about that side. He wants the nice obedient girl in Jami. But why?

"Anyway, I want you and everyone to have fun tonight, and I appreciate you all helping us out like this."

"Free drinks and food," I begin as he leans in and we do that guy hug thing, you know where you fist each other's hand, and tap each other on the back. "I'm the one who should be thanking you." The front door opens, and I go perfectly still.

"Dude, are you okay?" Kellan asks.

"What?" I ask absentmindedly.

"You just groaned."

"Oh, I didn't even realize I did."

He stands back and eyes me and I hope he can't see the way my pants are tenting. "Are you in pain or something?"

"Or something," I answer.

He turns to see what caught my attention and when his eyes land on Jami, dressed as a sexy Betty, he covers his eyes and steps back. "Nope, nope. Don't want to see that."

I laugh and clap his back, and turn him to point him toward Brad, who is watching us. "I think someone wants to say hello. But you'll need to open your eyes." He does and when he sees Brad, he grins.

"Thanks, Kai." He walks away and I turn back to Jami. My God, is she trying to kill me? The room grows silent before me, nothing existing but Jami as she walks toward me. From the corner of my eye, I spot Bree watching us, but then her attention is diverted as Brennan hurries over to her. My gaze goes back to Jami.

"Hey," is all I manage to utter as my dick twitches. She closes the distance between us, and the second I get a whiff of her sweet cucumber scent, I'm pretty sure I'm going to take her right here on one of the tables.

She looks a bit shy, unsure of herself in her shortened skirt and blouse that's tied just below her breast to expose the silky-smooth skin of her midriff. While I loved her—*loved her?*—in the outfit the way it was, I really love this version.

"It was Summer and Bree's idea," she explains, like she's suddenly unsure of the whole thing. She glances down and frowns. "Is it okay? I mean—"

"Yes, it is," I tell her. "In fact, it's so okay that I am losing my goddamn mind." I put my hands on her waist, and she takes a little breath as I spread my fingers, wanting to touch all her warm skin. "Sexy Betty," I murmur. "Sexy Jami."

"I don't think anyone has ever called me sexy before," she admits.

"For the record, I like this." I run the soft material on her shirt through my fingers and moan. "But I liked you in the old version too."

There's a gleam in her eye as she points toward the door. "Oh, do you want me to go back—"

"Fuck no."

She laughs, and I slide my arm around her waist, and while we haven't really been doing public displays of affection around the team, it must be clear to them all what is really happening here. I pull her to me, hard, letting her know, in no uncertain terms what she does to me, and plant my lips on hers. I kiss her deeply, and ignore the howls around me as I delve into the depths of her mouth Someone yells, telling us to get a room and I'd damn well plan to do that later, if I don't take her in the bathroom first. The thought has crossed my mind. Actually, a lot of thoughts are currently crossing my mind. Thoughts that make me happy, and thoughts that scare the living hell out of me.

The sound of silverware hitting a glass draws our attention. We turn to find Kellan standing near the bar. "Welcome everyone. I want to thank you all for helping me out tonight.

Please find a seat and make yourself comfortable. There are menus in front of you, and you will be served four courses. Our servers will be around to take your orders. So please seat yourselves and let's get this party started."

He finishes speaking and spooky music plays in the background. I take Jami's hand in mine. "Kai, Jami, over here," Brennan calls, and we walk around those pairing up for their tables, and slide in across from our friends.

Bree smiles at me. "What do you think of Jami's costume?" she asks.

"I think you are a very good design student." I say and put my hand on Jami's thigh under the table. Her entire body quivers, and my cock twitches.

"If I'd known you were going to be a cavegirl, I would have come as a caveman," Brennan says.

She laughs and bumps against him. "You don't have to dress up, Brennan. You're already a caveman."

He laughs. "Does that mean I can put you over my shoulder and carry you out of here?" he asks and I'm pretty sure he's only half joking.

Bree's gaze moves to Jami and they exchange a look I don't understand. Then it hits me, and yes, I guess I am stunned. Jami and Brennan both asked about my feelings for Bree. Is it because she likes me? Oh, fuck. The last thing I want to do is hurt her. She's my friend, and I could never forgive myself.

Isn't this why you don't get close, Kai? Because you could hurt the people you love.

I stiffen, and as if sensing my sudden unease, Jami puts her hand over mine, giving it a reassuring squeeze.

Bree smiles and turns back to Brennan. "How about we finish the four courses and then we'll see if you can still lift me."

Brennan laughs. "Oh babe, you're on."

Bree catches me staring and she gives me a warm smile, and I think she's telling me she gets it. That we'll only ever be friends, and I relax a bit. Bree and Brennan actually make a great couple. I lift my head as the server comes and spot Brad chatting with Kellan. They are so totally into each other, it's cute. Honestly, everything about tonight is so perfect it's almost scary.

I turn to take in my teammates, and the girls—my people. A new, unfamiliar kind of warmth spreads through my chest as I glance around, my gaze straying to the decorated restaurant window, where cobwebs and spiders threaten to overtake us. My gaze zeroes in on movement behind the decorations. What the fuck. Is that fucking douche bag looking at us from the sidewalk? Was he the one lurking in the shadows?

I stand quickly, my chair almost falling backward. "I'll be right back."

JAMI

I can't fight down the butterflies swarming in my stomach, knowing Kai is at evaluation camp and his chance at the future he wants could come to fruition this weekend. His last message came in hours ago, and he was excited and nervous, and I'm assuming I haven't heard from him since because he's out there giving it his all.

"He's going to do just fine," Brennan says from across the table at their favorite pub, and I set my phone down. It kind of feels weird to be here with all Kai's friends when he's not here, but Bree and Summer came and collected me from my house, refusing to let me spend a Friday night alone. Tomorrow, I head back to Greenwood to work at the resource center, and I'm sure the kids are going to be asking about Kai. Next weekend, however, is Thanksgiving and we'll be traveling together then. I'm actually counting down the days, even though I have a big test to write the day I get back. Why do professors want us studying on our holiday weekend?

My phone pings and everyone stares at it. I love how much Kai's friends support him and are all looking forward to hearing more from Edmonton. I pick it up and while I was hoping it was Kai, I'm not disappointed that it's my mom. Over the last week, we've talked more, and our relationship has changed a bit, for the better. All thanks to Kai. God, he is so good for me.

"It's my mother," I explain and everyone exhales and leans back in their seats. I read the text and my stomach twists inside out. "What the hell?" I mutter under my breath.

Bree puts her hand on my arm. "Is everything okay?"

"Yes," I answer, and shake my head, which is contradictory to my words. "I just uh…my parents, well, our whole family, are invited out to dinner tomorrow night."

"That sounds nice."

It would sound nice, if it wasn't at the base commander's house. What the hell is Theo up to? Of course, my father isn't going to say no to the base commander. I plaster on a smile and note the nervous way Bree is watching me. My stomach clenches, because I don't want to hurt her.

"Kai seems very happy, Jami."

I swallow. "Does he?"

"Yes, and you seem happy too."

For the first time in a long time, I am happy and I feel pretty crappy about that. "You really like him, huh?" she asks.

"I'm sorry," I blurt out.

She shakes her head. "Hey, the heart wants what the heart wants. We don't always have a choice in that."

"But you like him. I've always known that. I never wanted to come between you guys. I just didn't think—"

"How could you not fall for him, Jami? He's a great guy."

As my throat grows tight, I agree. "I know."

"He's different now, though. Happier. It's because of you."

"Bree…"

"It's okay. See, I really care about Kai, and if you're what makes him happy, then that makes me happy." She smiles. "Besides, I've kind of been getting to know Brennan a little better, if you know what I mean."

My eyes go wide. "I think I do."

She laughs. "We went to his family's cottage in Chester Basin last weekend. I had no idea he could be so romantic." She leans in. "Just don't tell him I said that." Another laugh and then, "The guys all put on a tough show, but there really are just cinnamon rolls underneath the jersey."

I laugh with her, and when it dies down, I go very serious. "You're okay with Kai and me?"

"More than okay. I have never seen him happier." She nibbles on her bottom lip and frowns.

"What?" I ask.

"I just…I'm not sure your ex is going to be okay with it. Wasn't this bet for one month? What happens then? I'm pretty sure he expects you to go back to him?" She glances around, like she expects Theo to be in a bar occupied by his rivals. "I actually think I've seen him around, watching you."

My stomach cramps because maybe he really was outside my brother's restaurant that night. Kai stormed out, only to find the sidewalk empty. Why would Theo be lurking? He was quick to let me go, to break up with me. Is he sorry? Was losing me a wakeup call? Does he want me back—exclusively?

"Maybe the better question is, are you planning to go back with him?" Bree asks.

"No," I say quickly. "It's over between us. Being with Kai, seeing how a woman should be treated." I groan and bury my face in my hands. "I'm ashamed, actually. I stayed in the relationship knowing how bad it was. I'm going to be a social worker. I should know better, Bree."

"Don't beat yourself up." There's warmth and understanding in her eyes as she takes my hands away from my face. "It's not always easy to leave."

"I know. I actually do know that sometimes it's harder to leave a bad relationship than stay in it." It takes courage and strength, none of which I had. But I'm not that girl anymore. Thanks to Kai, I've changed and while I agreed to the bet because I had my own agenda, I'm not really sure Theo has changed.

"It's kind of nice when the hottest guy in your school, the captain of the hockey team, wants you though, right?"

I groan at her very astute observation. The truth is, and we all know it, that I'm not the kind of girl Theo's been with since he moved to the city. "Am I that pathetic?"

"No, Jami. You're human, with real feelings and needs." She reaches for the pitcher of beer and pours me a glass. "Have another drink. I think you need it."

She pours us both a drink and we clink glasses and when she smiles at me, it makes me hate myself less, because I never wanted to hurt her.

"Hey Bree, get over here," Brennan calls, and she stands, walks around to the other side of the table, and he pulls her onto his lap. Something in the way he looks at her is really sweet. She's right. Underneath the jersey, the guys are all cinnamon rolls, and I just happen to like sweet things. But that reminds me of Kai again, telling me how he liked sweet things. My entire body quivers, and when my phone pings again, I reach for it, and smile when I see that it's from Kai, telling me he's kicking ass.

"He's kicking ass, you guys."

Cheers erupt around the table and for the next hour, we all happily chat and I settle in, joining in conversations, and really loving being a part of this amazing group. Soon enough, it's bedtime, and Brennan and Bree walk me home. Apparently, Kai asked Brennan to make sure I get home safe and that seriously warms my heart.

I wave to them from my door, and head straight up to bed, dreading dinner tomorrow. Maybe it's all a mistake and I read it wrong. In the months Theo and I have been together, his parents had never invited us to their place before. Of course, he's not been to mine either, but my parents knew about him. Strange they didn't ask too many questions when I showed up with Kai. I walk to my bathroom to get washed up, then head to my bed. I throw myself down, missing Kai's touch.

I reach for my phone, and once again consider telling Kai about tomorrow's dinner. Maybe I'll wait. He's at evaluation camp and I don't want to say anything that could throw him off his game. Also, maybe I won't go, or if I do, perhaps the commander is having a big party and I can fade into the background. My parents want my presence, but that doesn't mean I have to be the center of attention or even talk to Theo. No sense in bringing it up if it's not going to be a big deal.

I fall into a restless sleep and wake to birds chirping. Which is good. I need to spend time on a paper I have due before I head home. I spend the morning working, and when I receive a text from Kai, my heart thuds. He's busy and unable to talk, but hopes we can connect later tonight, before lights out. By the time I finish my paper, it's mid-afternoon, and I pack up and get in my car. It's a nice drive home, especially with all the gorgeous fall foliage.

I ease into our driveway, and smile at the wreath on the door. I hurry inside, and call out to Mom and Dad. I find them in the kitchen and a smile lights their faces when they see me.

"Doesn't Kellan have to come to this dinner too?" I ask.

"Oh, honey, you know Kellan is busy with the restaurant."

"I know, but what is this all about anyway?" I drop down into a chair and Mom grabs me a cup of coffee. "Thanks."

"We thought you might know," Dad says and scrubs his chin.

I sit up a bit straighter. Dammit, this is about me, then. "Are you and Theo still..." Mom begins.

I take a big drink of coffee and let it burn down my throat. How do I tell them he gave me away in a bet, or worse, I let him. I have my own mind and voice. I could have said or done something right. But no, I had an agenda of my own.

"It's complicated," I finally say as they watch me.

"Because of Kai?" Dad asks.

I nod. "Yes, because of Kai. We're sort of together." For a month, but they don't need to know that, and honestly, I want more than a month. The problem is, I don't know what Kai wants. I also don't know what Theo is up to. "He's away at an evaluation camp this weekend," I tell them excitedly.

Mom reaches out and takes Dad's hand. "You and Theo broke up?"

"Something like that?"

Dad eyes me. He's astute and obviously knows I'm telling half-truths. "I think Theo thinks we're getting back together."

"What do you want, Jami?" Mom asks, and I turn to her, take in her very serious expression. I'm not sure my mother has ever asked what I wanted before. Or maybe she has and I just assumed it was because she needed me alive and well for my brother.

"What?" I ask, for lack of anything else.

"We want what is best for you." Her hand closes over mine. "We want you to be happy. That's all we have ever wanted for you and Kellan."

I smile at her, and think about how protective she is, not just because I was born to save my brother, but because she loves me, and worries about me. Kai helped me see that.

"I'm not sure Theo and I were ever a good fit."

"We won't go tonight," Dad announces, planting his palms on the table in a manner that says this is all settled, but I know he can't do that. When the base commander invites you to his house for dinner, you go to the base commander's house for dinner. It's disrespectful not to, and I refuse to do anything that might impact his career. But it warms me that he would do this for me. They really do love me.

"No, we're going," I decide and square my shoulders. "I'm an adult, and I can't hide from Theo forever. We'll have a nice meal, and talk. Then later, I will make it perfectly clear to Theo that we're over for good."

Mom pats my hand. "Good for you, Jami. Don't ever be afraid to go after what you want, and you can't stay in a relationship if that relationship isn't working for you."

I knew for a long time it wasn't working, but I held on until Kai helped me open my eyes. Theo must know we're not right for each other. Heck, he rarely wanted me around when he was with his friends, and that begs the question, why is he clinging to it?

"You should have been a social worker," I tease and Mom laughs.

"Call me old-fashioned, but I enjoyed staying home with you and Kellan. That was the only job I ever wanted."

"Thanks, Mom," I tell her, standing to give her a hug. I give Dad one too. "I'd better go shower and get ready." I head to my room and check my phone to see if Kai messaged. I shoot off a text wishing him good luck and then spend the rest of my time getting ready for dinner. Back in my room, I read a few messages from Bree, Summer and a few of the other girls. I love how they added me to their group chat. For the first time ever, I feel like I belong somewhere, and that some-where is not beside Theo or at his family's dinner table, but I'm a grown woman and I'm going to act like it.

I shoot a message to Jim to make sure Mila is covering for me. I let him know last night I wouldn't be available, but I'd rather be at the resource center than at Theo's place. Maybe if dinner is over fast, I can head to the center.

An hour later, I find myself walking down the street with my parents. The commander's house isn't too far, and it's a nice night, so we opted for a walk, and I don't want to drive, because I'm pretty sure I'll need a glass or two of something to get me through the night.

We reach the Wagner's house, which is decorated beautifully for fall and Halloween. The door opens before we can knock and we're greeted with a big smile from Jessica Wagner, Theo's beautiful mom. I've seen her around plenty, but we've never been formally introduced. My parents naturally know her from functions over the years.

She ushers us inside and after introductions and hugs, we're led to the living room. Theo's father Blake stands and shakes our hands and I spot Theo standing behind him, and while he's clean cut and well dressed, there's something very different—very formal—about him.

Blake, dressed similar to Dad in nice pants and a button-down shirt, smiles at me. "Jami, Theo has told us so much about you. It's well past time that we met. Please come in and sit."

Theo had told them so much about me?

Blake steps to the side and Theo moves forward, gently putting his hand on my back, and guiding me to the sofa. Blake waves to matching recliners and Mom and Dad sit.

Jessica smiles at us. "Dinner will be ready soon. In the meantime, what can I get you all to drink?"

"Well, you know your son and I will have a scotch," Blake says. "How about you, Derek?"

"Sounds good to me," Dad agrees. "Can I help?"

Blake looks almost aghast. He waves a dismissive hand. "No need."

Jessica smiles at Blake in a very worshipping way, before turning to Mom. "Wine? I have red or white."

"White is great and that's a lot to carry. Let me help."

This time Blake doesn't speak up, and it's easy to tell, like my family, that Theo's parents have very traditional roles.

Jessica gives Mom a grateful smile. "That would be lovely."

"I hear you've been scouted, Theo," my dad says after Mom and Jessica go into the other room.

"We're very proud of him," Blake replies with a smile and a nod. "And you, Jami. You're in the social work program. Theo tells me you want to work with military families."

Wow, I wasn't even sure he listened when I told him that.

"I do," I agree.

"Very good. Once you have a family, though, I'm sure you'll prefer to be at home."

His remark takes me by surprise. Why would he be sure of that? I open my mouth to correct him, or at least tell him my future plans aren't set in stone. I have no idea if I'll stay at home or even if I'm going to have kids, when Jessica pokes her head in.

"Jami, I do apologize. I just assumed you would like a glass of white."

I nod. "Sounds great." What I really want to say is, make it a big one.

Mom comes in carrying the scotch on a tray and she hands them out. Jessica follows her with the wine. Our parents talk for a second and once there's a break in conversation, Theo straightens his back and looks at his father.

"Would it be okay if I showed Jami the pool before dinner?"

His father nods. "Of course, son."

"Thank you, sir."

What the heck? He calls his father sir? That's so very formal. I mean, I get things are formal when you're the base commander, but this is his son.

I snatch up my purse and Theo holds his hand out to me, and guides me from the stuffy room and once we're outside, he lets out a breath.

"Are you okay?"

He turns to me and smiles. "Thanks for coming."

I take a big drink of wine, fueling myself for this conversation. "What is this all about?"

He steps into me and brushes my hair back. "I wanted my parents to meet you, baby. I've missed you. Have you missed me too? I was stupid to agree to the bet. I've been counting down the days until you're back with me."

"Theo, we need to talk." His dark eyes turn cold as they narrow in on me. Before he can say anything, my phone rings and I inch back and pull it from my purse. My heart jumps when I see it's Kai, and I debate on answering it. I don't want him to think I'm ignoring him and I'm not sure when I'll hear from him again so I slide my finger across the screen.

"Hi," I say, suddenly breathless. I lift my gaze, and from the scowl on Theo's face, it's clear he knows who I'm talking to.

"Jami," he says and wherever he is, the music is so loud, I press my hand to my other ear, struggling to hear. "I did so great today."

"I'm so happy to hear that."

"Hey, are you okay? You sound strange. Are your allergies bothering you again?"

I breathe deeply. "Actually no. I'm good."

"Glad to hear it. You must be getting ready to head to the resource center."

"Ah, actually—" I steal a glance at Theo as he steps closer, and brace myself.

"Let me refill your wine." Theo says, his grin twisted spitefully as he takes my glass from me.

"Who the fuck was that?" Kai asks, and my heart jumps into my throat.

"It was...Theo." Oh God, this looks so bad. "I'm at his parent's place."

A beat of silence as music and voices blare in the background. "I go away for one weekend and you're with Theo?"

"Kai...it's not what you think."

"No, then what am I supposed to think?"

"Kai, come on," some girl yells in the background and then, before I can tell him what he's supposed to think, or ask who the girl is, he adds, "I guess you're not allergic to him."

I grip my phone tighter. "Kai, please."

"I have to go."

He disconnects and I catch Theo smirking at me. He leans in, looking nothing like the poised, obedient man he presents to his father. "He's not who you think he is, Jami. You're nothing but a bet to him. He's using you. You're a pawn, and when the month is over, maybe even before that, he's going to toss you away." I glare at him and he grins and adds, "Don't worry, I'll let you back in my bed."

KAI

I stare out at the clouds as we approach Stanfield Airport, just outside of Halifax. I feel sick to my stomach. Not because I played shitty at evaluation camp, I didn't, and not because I drank too much last night, which I did. I'm ill because Jami was with Theo at his fucking house, and I only found out because I called her earlier than she expected.

What the fuck though, man? What was going on? Of course, I could have stayed on the phone a bit longer and found out, but Christ, anger hit hard and fast, not to mention old hurts of love and loss came back to haunt me, and I shut the conversation down. Yeah, I'm an idiot, and I own that.

I haven't messaged her since, because dammit, texting can get fucked up and I want to talk to her in person, see her face when she explains why she was with that douche bag. I swallow against a tight throat and a garbled noise crawls out of my mouth as I try to shift in my seat. They're so fucking small, it's impossible to get comfortable.

I rest my head against the seat, but that doesn't help because there's a small child behind me kicking my seat. I grip the armrests and take deep breaths, so goddamn anxious to get off this fucking plane, I'm ready to explode.

I check my phone again to see if Jami sent any messages, and I try not to visualize her at Theo's parent's house. What the fuck, man. I still can't wrap my brain around it, and when I try, I get images of the two of them together that turn me into a raging caveman. There has to be an explanation. Jami is sweet and kind and I was sure she felt the same things for me that I felt for her.

Could I have been wrong?

No, I'm not wrong, and I deserve to be tortured for hanging up on her, and not giving her the chance to explain. Stupid bastard. I'll be lucky if she even talks to me when I get back. The landing gears starts to lower, signaling our approach, and I start tapping the armrest. I count down the minutes and as soon as we touch down, I unbuckle my seatbelt, even though I'm not supposed to and get ready to bolt as soon as the doors open.

With my nerves firing, I grab my bag from the overhead bin, and wait in the aisle. Since I'm in the front row, I'm able to exit the second the doors open.

"Thanks," I say to the flight attendant as I barrel past her. I head to oversized baggage and wait impatiently for mt gear. When it finally arrives, I head down the escalator and straight outside, to where my jeep is waiting in the parking lot. I toss my gear into the back, pay for parking and hit the highway, praying to fuck that Jami is back from the valley, and willing to talk to me.

I don't drive home. I go straight to Jami's place, and pound on the door. Her roommate finally answers, and seems a bit shocked to see me on the stoop. Probably because I look like a crazed lunatic.

"She's not here," she says with a smile that holds all kinds of suggestions. "But if you want to come in and wait."

Jesus.

"Do you know where she is?"

She shrugs. "Nope."

My stomach knots harder. "Is she back from the valley?"

"I don't keep track of her movements."

"Well, maybe you should," I shoot back and her mouth drops open. I don't mean to be rude, but what kind of a friend is she? Aren't women, especially roommates, supposed to look out for one another? Hell, I looked out for Coop and he looked out for me, and there isn't a guy on my team who wouldn't help me out if I needed it.

I jump back in my car, and head to my place. As soon as I get there and find a quiet spot, I plan to call Jami. I need to find out where she is and if she'll agree to see me, or at least talk to me. As I drive through town, my chest is so tight it's almost hard to breathe. Did I fuck this up between us?

It's dark and the streets are quiet, but I try not to speed. I flick on my signal, and pull down my street, slowing as a couple walks their dog in front of my driveway. Once they've passed, I ease in, and my headlights splash against the stoop, highlighting a slumped figure on the steps.

Jami.

My door is open before I barely get the jeep into park, and I hurry across the walkway to find her sitting there, hugging herself. "Jami," I whisper as she tightens her arms around her body to ward off the chill. I reach for her, and pull her to me to keep her warm. "How long have you been here."

"Not that long," she answers, but I'm not sure if I believe her.

"What...what are you doing?" I guide her up the steps and grab my key from my pocket. "Did you knock?"

"I did but Thomas must be out."

"I went to your place," I tell her and she relaxes a bit.

Surprise lights her face. "You did?"

"Yes, we need to talk."

She blinks up at me with big blue eyes that hold fear and vulnerability. "That's why I'm here." I push my door open and pull her inside, so happy we're on the same page.

I cup her face, and press my lips to hers, desperate to kiss her and make things right between us. "Babe," I begin. "I'm so sorry. I was an asshole. I thought the worst, and I knew better than to do that."

"You were an asshole," she agrees and I chuckle into her mouth as I devour her with my lips.

"Tell me I didn't fuck this up."

"No, you didn't and you're not the only one at fault. You're my boyfriend," she eyes me, like she's gauging my reaction to that one word.

"Boyfriend," I whisper.

I'm her boyfriend.

She lets loose a breath. "I didn't want to upset you while you were at camp, and I wasn't sure why my parents and I were invited to Theo's parents place for dinner. I only know that when the base commander asks your family to dinner, there's no choice but to go. But I should have given you the heads up."

"Speaking of up." I nod to the stairs, needing her in my room, my bed, more than I need my next breath. She nods and I take her hand. We hurry to my room and I lock the door behind us. As soon as we get inside, she sneezes. I frown. Maybe she really is allergic to me.

"Theo's parents," she begins and I shake my head to stop her, as I take my jacket off and toss it over my chair. She angles her head, confused.

"I know you're cold." I grip her zipper. "But if you take this off, I promise to warm you all over."

She gulps and nods, and I slide the zipper down and ease the jacket from her shoulders. I glance at her perfect body, hidden behind a baggy sweater and jeans with holes in the knees, and my cock thickens. "I missed you."

"I missed you too."

I step into her, and slide my hands under her sweater and moan as my fingers connect with her soft skin.

"Kai," she whispers, her head falling forward onto my shoulder.

"You missed this?" I ask, as I slide my hands around her back to unhook her bra.

She juts her chest out as I slide my hand beneath the loose cups and palm her supple breasts. Her moan curls around me, and my cock aches as it presses against my jeans. I find her lips again, and kiss her with all my pent-up hunger. I know absence makes the heart grow fonder, but it's only been one weekend.

She reaches down and opens the button on my jeans, and the sound of my zipper hissing open reaches my ears. I yelp as she slides her small hand into my boxers. "Jesus, your hand is cold," I tell her.

She grins and pulls her hand out, blowing on it. "Fuck," I swear as she puckers her lips and I imagine them on another part of my body. A grin tugs at her lips as she drops to her knees, clearly reading my mind.

"My hands are cold but my mouth is warm."

"Jami..."

She tugs my jeans and boxers down just enough to release my cock. She lightly strokes me, her breath warm on my flesh when she glances up and asked, "Did you miss this?"

"Yeah, babe, I missed this. I...missed you." For the briefest of seconds, the word love dances on my tongue, but I'm not sure she wants to hear that and I don't want to do or say anything else that might mess things up between us. She leans forward and takes me to the back of her throat and all coherent thought packs a bag and heads south.

Heaven, pure fucking heaven.

"Babe," I murmur, and push her hair to the side, loving the way she moves her body, taking pleasure from pleasuring me. It's the most sensual, beautiful thing I've ever seen. My heart skips a beat as I simply watch her, admire every single thing about her as she works my cock with her sweet mouth.

I thicken even more, and I have to work to stay standing on shaky legs as she twirls her tongue around my crown, lapping at my pre-cum and while I want this to continue, I need it to stop. "Jami," I manage to get out. "I need you naked. I need my cock inside you."

"Yes please," she responds, her words rushed and shaky... excited. I pull her to her feet, and slide my hands under her sweater again. She lifts her arms and moans as I peel it from her body, tossing her sweater and bra on my chair, but then her face twists and her eyes go wide. Christ, is she having second thoughts about this? Us? Maybe I should have let her talk.

"Jami," I murmur and she steps back, turning from me and sneezes into her elbow. "Oh, babe," I murmur and she hurries to her coat to grab a tissue.

She gazes at me with watery, apologetic eyes. "I'm sorry. This is hardly sexy."

"Are you kidding me." God, she looks so adorable it hurts my heart. "Even your sneezes are sexy."

"Liar," she shoots back, and I hold my arms out to her.

"Come here."

She steps into me, and I put my arms around her back and spread my fingers. Picking up right where we left off, her hips move suggestively as she rubs up against me, and I back up an inch to tear my clothes off.

"Fast," she chuckles, as I reach for her pants, eager to get her naked.

I grin as desire reflects in her eyes. "You know I can be slow."

"Maybe I don't want that tonight."

With that, I make quick work of her pants and panties as she moans and she reaches for my hard cock. She strokes me and I back her up, until she's sitting on the bed. I easily move her to the middle and crawl between her legs. The second I taste her, her flavor exploding in my mouth, I let loose a groan of pleasure, happy to be back where I belong.

"I missed your taste," I moan and swirl my tongue over her swollen clit. Her hips lift as she offers herself to me and I happily take everything she's willing to give. Would she offer her heart? I don't know, but what I do know is she's currently offering me her body and I plan to cherish it.

I slide a finger into her tight channel and she quivers around me. My cock throbs as her wet heat soaks my skin, and I move my finger around to prepare her, even though she's writhing and begging, completely ready for me. I fucking love it.

We haven't bothered with condoms since that time I got carried away and forgot it, so I climb over her body, and she wraps her arms around me holding me tight, like she never wants to let me go, and I don't want her to. I'm in deep, and it's scary. So, fucking scary.

I move my hips forward and inch my cock into her and her sex clenches around me. She's already so close but I have no room to talk. I'm seconds from exploding on impact. She lifts her body and I slide all the way inside, finding her mouth with mine as we move together in sync.

Her nails scratch down my back, and I slide my hands under her shoulders for leverage and I move in and out of her hot, wet tightness. Her legs wrap around me and we're holding on to one another like our lives depend on it.

"Kai," she murmurs, her body tightening beneath me and I rock into her as she gives herself over to her climax. Her hot heat sears my cock, bringing on my own orgasm, and I push high and go still inside her as I fill her with my seed. "Yes," she murmurs as I bury my face in her neck and press hot, hungry, open-mouthed kisses to her damp skin. How is it I can never get enough of her?

With my cock still inside her, I collapse on top of her, shifting a bit, so I don't crush her beneath me. I brush the hair from her forehead and the smile she gives me curls around my heart and squeezes.

"That was better than fighting about douche bag," I tell her.

"Much, and totally makes up for you being an asshole."

I laugh at that and my cock slides from her body as I roll. "Didn't you claim some of the blame, too?"

"Yes," she agrees and stretches her arms, a happy contented smile on her face. "And I did my part here too."

"Yeah, you did babe. I'll be right back."

I climb from the bed and since no one is home, I hurry to the bathroom naked and wash myself down. I grab a cloth to clean Jami and turn the water to hot. Once I soak the cloth, I give it a squeeze, and turn the tap off. That's when I hear Jami sneezing, loudly and repeatedly. Dammit, what is going on? I rush back to my bedroom, and that's when I see Mittens has found her way into my room and she's currently sitting on the bed, engaging Jami in a staring contest.

"Mittens," I yell. "Get out."

Mittens meows at me, glancing at my dick like it's a scratching post and I throw the washcloth over it. "Don't even think about it."

She lifts her tail, as if to say *fuck you*, jumps from the bed and scurries into the hall. Jami laughs as I slam the door shut and continue to protect my dick. "What? That cat is unpredictable and sketchy as hell."

She shakes her head at me. "I didn't know you had a cat. It explains so much."

"Thomas's cat. A rescue. Let me guess, you're allergic."

"Highly," she answers and sneezes again.

"At least we got to the bottom of that. But I guess that means you don't have to repeatedly expose yourself to me. No immunotherapy?"

She pushes her blankets off to showcase her gorgeous naked body and crooks her finger. "You guessed wrong. Get your cute butt over here, boyfriend."

It's been one week since Kai came back from evaluation camp and I am so happy how that night ended. I figured we were over, and while he trusted me enough that he didn't want to hear why I was at Theo's, I told him anyway. What I didn't tell him, or anyone for that matter, was how seeing Theo with his family gave me a bit of insight into what makes him tick—and it's not good.

For years, Theo was the perfect son, at least on the surface, while we were living in Greenwood. We never hung out because I was never in his circle, or any circle for that matter. But when we went to the city, to Kingston—and he was away from his father's eye—he let loose, dating all the puck bunnies and partying every weekend. That's why I was surprised when he walked me home that night, and called me the next day.

Now though, now I'm beginning to wonder if his father told him to find a nice girl, an obedient woman, one who is going to stay home and take care of the family while he's away being the NHL star. I swallow down the sudden lump in my throat.

Honestly, to think he only wanted to be with me because I checked his father's boxes, makes me ill, and lets me know I was a means to an end, that I was being used, a pawn. Much like I felt growing up. He twisted the story, telling me I was nothing but a pawn for Kai, but I'm pretty sure that's all I have ever been to Theo.

No wonder Theo never wanted me around after games. He wanted to party with his friends and I was in the way. I don't even want to know what he was doing with the puck bunnies, but it had to be lots, considering how rarely he touched me.

"You're quiet," Kai says, and I turn to him as he drives us to the valley in his jeep.

I laugh and push down my dark thoughts. They're not worth dwelling on. Especially when I'm heading home with a man I'm falling for. "Just thinking about all the turkey we have to eat these next two days."

The base is putting on its annual Thanksgiving Day dinner at the mess hall, and everyone is invited. It's always loud and chaotic, and while I'd be happy to miss it, Mom and Dad like me there, and—big news—Kellan is coming with Brad. I'm so happy the two are hitting it off. Kai offered to go with me, and I'm pretty happy about that, too.

"Turkey in the mess hall tonight, and then turkey tomorrow with my parents."

"We'll be in for a big nap after all that," I joke.

He snorts out a laugh. "A date nap sounds just about right." He leans forward, and checks the sky. I know he hates driving on this two-lane highway after dark, but it's only midafternoon.

He casts me a fast glance, his eyes hopeful. "Do you think we have time to stop?"

"Sure." I eye him and he has a mischievous look on his face. "What are you up to, Ward?"

"Me?" He whistles innocently and my insides soar. He's so sweet and so much fun to be with. How did I ever get so lucky? We only have one week left in our arrangement, and neither of us have brought that up. I plan to, though. I want more, and I think he does too. It might have started as a bet, and we both had our own agendas, but I'm sure there is more going on here, now

I reach across the seat and put my hand on his lap. He shifts uncomfortably. "Keep touching me like that and I'll pull off and take you right here."

"Maybe I'd like that."

"Jesus," he curses and I can't help but laugh at the tortured sound. Honestly, I love the way he is around me, the way I get him worked up without even trying. I touch the necklace dangling around my neck. I can't believe he brought me home a souvenir from Edmonton. He apologized for getting it at the airport because he didn't have time to shop, but I love it so much. Theo never gave me gifts—not that I need gifts— but it's the fact that he thought about me when he was away that touches the deepest parts of my heart. Theo has no idea what he's talking about. Why would Kai bring me something back if I was nothing but a pawn? I mean, unless he did it to really piss Theo off.

Okay, why is Theo living rent free in my brain, his warning words bouncing around like a runaway pinball? Oh, maybe because there's still a part of me that worries that I—Jami

Nichols—have no value other than what I can do for other people.

His gaze moves to my hand as I play with the charm, and a warm smile touches his mouth. I turn back to stare out the window, and he takes the next exit. I sit up. "Where exactly are we going?"

He doesn't speak, he just keeps driving and when he pulls into Dempsey's farm, I start laughing. "We're apple picking."

"I do owe you a bag, don't I?"

"Yeah, you do," I tell him. "I forgot about that."

He smiles at me. "We're not just apple picking," he tells me and points to the children's play area, where chickens and goats run free as the kids play on the equipment.

"I think you're too big to climb on that merry-go-round, Kai. You'll crush it."

He laughs. "Did I tell you that I make an apple pie every year for Thanksgiving?"

"Are you serious. You bake?"

"Not well, but it was my one job, and I kind of enjoyed it," he admits almost shyly. "I actually haven't done it in a couple of years, but I want to this year. Will you help me this year?"

My heart pinches tight. I love that he's back to doing things he loves, things that bring him pleasure. "Of course. I'm not much of a baker either, but you can teach me."

He eases his jeep between two big SUVs, and I step out and take a deep breath. "There is nothing better than the smell of apples," I say as he crosses in front of the jeep and takes my hands. We head into the barn to get a big plastic bag for the apples, and we're told to head up the hill to the back of the orchard where the golden delicious variety are growing. I'm totally out of breath by the time we make the trek to the top, but the view from high up is simply gorgeous.

I drop down beneath the tree and lean against it. Kai pulls off an apple, shines it on his shirt, and sits next to me. He takes a big bite of his apple, and hands it to me. We sit quietly for about five minutes, enjoying the view, the company, and the juicy apple.

I catch him checking the time again, and I push to my feet. "Ready?"

He stands, puts one hand around my neck and backs me up against the tree. He presses his body against me, and his mouth finds mine. He moans as he kisses me, and between his legs, his thickening cock lets me know he's totally ready.

In the distance, we hear children laughing and I break the kiss, even though I don't want to. "If we don't cut it out, we're going to get arrested for public indecency."

"You're not wrong. But I really want you naked."

"Too risky."

"I know you like risks, but yeah, I get it." He steps back, adjusts his pants, and glances up. "I know you want to climb it."

"More than anything, but I think they want us to use the ladders, and I don't want to fall and break my neck before I get my two turkey dinners."

He swallows and admits, "I don't really want you to climb it anyway."

It's clear he's still scared of so many things.

"If I did, and if by some unforeseen circumstances I fell, I know you'd catch me." He blinks at me, and I add, "But we'd better not risk it." While I can be a risk taker, he's not. Not after the accident, and since I didn't know him before it, I'm not sure what he was like previously. He walks over to get the ladder and I sigh with pleasure as I take in his tight backside.

"I know you're looking," he teases without even turning my way and I laugh.

"I'm allowed to look at my boyfriend."

He picks up the ladder, and let's his gaze move down the length of me. "As long as I'm allowed to look at my girlfriend."

Butterflies take flight in my stomach. "Of course, and later, if you play your cards right, I'll let you look without clothes on."

He groans. "Let's get these fucking apples and get out of here." He braces the ladder against the tree.

"I'll go first."

I climb, and pick the biggest apples and hand them to him. I can't believe he had this planned, and how much fun I'm having with him. Theo is so wrong about Kai. He is exactly who I think he is.

"Do you want to take a turn?" I ask. "The view of the valley is even better up here on the ladder."

"No, I'd rather stand here on the ground, with your ass in my face."

My head jerks down to see him. "What?" I ask, not sure if he's kidding until a big smile parts his gorgeous lips, lips that I really want to kiss again.

He puts his hands on my ass and gives a squeeze. I yelp and he laughs. "Trust me, the view is better from down here."

I reach for a couple more apples and when the bag is full enough, I climb down. "How are we doing for time?" I ask as he checks his phone.

He wags his eyebrows and puts one arm around me. "Time for one more thing."

"I told you, we're not getting naked in the orchard," I tease.

"Is that all you ever think about?" He feigns annoyance. "There's more to me than that, you know."

I whack his chest. "Oh please."

Laughing, we start down the big hill and he guides me to the children's area. He sets the bag of apples down as I glance around, unable to figure out what it is he wants to do. He puts his hands on my shoulders and turns me and a yelp of laughter rises in my throat when I see the children's axe throwing game—using Velcro axes of course.

"No way," I laugh.

"One of these days we'll make it to one of the axe throwing lounges in the city, but this is just to give you some practice."

"You are crazy."

"Jami," I turn at the sound of my name and go still when I see Mrs. Wagner—Theo's mom—standing on the other side of the small gate, a bag of produce in her hands. "I thought that was you."

"Oh hi, Mrs. Wagner." Her gaze leaves me and curiosity, mixed with something that looks like anger, dances in her eyes as she takes in my boyfriend. "This is Kai—"

"Ward," she snaps cutting me off and finishing my sentence, a new kind of hardness in her eyes. Jeez, maybe she's not as sweet as I thought she was. My gaze goes back and forth between the two of them as Kai stiffens.

I step closer to Kai, and when Mrs. Wagner turns to me, I say, "I didn't realize you two knew each other."

"Theo played against Kai many times over the years," she explains with a strained smile. "Rival schools." She waves her hand. "But you must know that."

"I...yeah, sure."

Her eyes are full of questions as they move over my face. Questions like why am I here with Kai and not her son.

She gives a fake laugh. "What is it Theo used to call you?" She taps her chin. "Oh, I remember. BM. What exactly does that stand for again?"

Kai stumbles back a bit, his face hard and full of rage. He opens his mouth, and I put my hand on his arm.

Before he can say a thing, Mrs. Wagner gives another wave of her hand. "Oh well, it doesn't matter. I'm running late, and must get going. I'll see you at the mess hall tonight." She turns and walks away, and both Kai and I stare after her. I shake my head, incredulous.

What the ever-loving hell just happened?

22

———

KAI

———

My insides have been a little raw since our run-in with the Wagner witch. All I was trying to do was pick some apples and throw an axe with Jami, wanting her to have fun, and Mrs. Wagner came along and with a few careless words, destroyed the day—destroyed me. It's insane to think how quickly she took me back to the night of the accident, to the pain and anger that I was learning to let go of, or at least deal with.

I don't believe for once second she doesn't know what those initials stand for. Theo hates me, and even more so now that I'm with Jami. Maybe I shouldn't have bet on her. Maybe I should have left well enough alone. That's the problem though, I took one look at Jami and knew she wasn't 'well enough'.

Still, maybe I'm getting into something I shouldn't be getting into. As old demons nip at my heels, I glance up from the long oaken table in the mess hall, and spot Jami watching me closely as she sits directly across from me. Theo and his family are somewhere in the room, and I really hope I don't run into them. I might do something I'll only regret later.

Jami's foot touches mine under the table and I do my best to give her a smile. Fuck, man, I shouldn't be letting that woman's words ruin this weekend. Jami and I have been looking forward to it for some time now. I take a deep breath and smile back at her, rubbing her foot with mine and she relaxes a bit.

"Kai," Jami's dad Derek begins as he holds out a basket of rolls. I accept one and put it on my plate. "I want to hear all about evaluation camp."

I laugh as big plates of food are set in front of us, and my stomach growls. "I don't want to bore everyone at the table," I reply, a lightness in my voice as I struggle to forget my encounter with Theo's mother.

"We'd love to hear," Jami says, and I just shake my head. I've told her every detail already, but I love how she's not bored with all my hockey talk.

"Come on, tell us," Kellan says and nudges me. I glance at him, and on the other side of him, Brad nods in agreement.

"You asked for it," I say and for the next half hour or so as we eat, I tell them all about my trip to Edmonton, the great players I met and how I think I have a pretty good chance of making it. "But the real talent at the table is Jami. Have you seen her curl?"

She laughs and once again nudges me with her foot under the table. "It's boring, I know."

"Far from it," I tell her and mean it. She could make painting a wall exciting.

"How can they call this turkey?" Kellan says and picks up a piece of dry turkey that could pass as the sole of a sneaker. "Someone let me in that kitchen."

Brad puts his hand on Kellan's arm. "No. Tonight is for relaxing. You spend too much time in the kitchen as it is, and you have a busy Christmas party season coming up."

Claire beams at Brad, who is clearly watching out for Kellan. Soon enough, the conversation turns to Brad, and how he plans to stay in the city after college. His goal is not the NHL, and he plans to put his business degree to use.

Our plates are cleared and dessert, consisting of pumpkin pie and whipped cream, is served and we all dig in. From the corner of my eye, I catch my roommate Thomas looking our way, and he has a very concerned expression on his face. What the hell is going on?

He stands, and gestures with a nod. "If you'll excuse me. I have to make a quick trip to the bathroom." I set my napkin on the table, not missing the curiosity on Jami's face as she watches me stand. I follow Thomas out into the hall, as he makes his way to the very end. He pushes through the bathroom door and I follow him in.

"What's up?" I ask.

"Have you seen Theo? He's been glaring at you all night." He scrubs his chin and starts pacing. "I don't like it."

"Theo can go fuck himself."

"I feel like he's up to something. He definitely doesn't like you here on his turf, with his girl."

I push my fingers through my hair and pace to the other side of the long bathroom. "She's not his girl, remember."

"Come on, Kai." He folds his arms and leans against the wall. "You know she is. Jesus, his father fucking picked her out for him. Everyone knows that."

My lungs seize. "What are you talking about?"

He shrugs. "I just thought…"

I knew that asshole had an agenda, I just didn't really know what it was, but the fact that his family was behind it… Jesus Christ, no wonder his mother was cruel today. She went into mama bear mode and was protecting her son, and what was best for him—which, according to them was Jami.

I cross my arms, before I hit something. "Why Jami?"

"You've met her. She's a good girl."

"The kind of girl they can push around, you mean. Obedient. Submissive." Fuck me twice. If Jami knew this, it would kill her. She can never hear this. It would make her feel worthless, like Theo only wanted her because she served a purpose.

"Hey, I didn't say that." He holds his hands up, palms out. "It's just you know, she comes from a good family, and grew up pretty sheltered. She's obedient, and everyone knows she was only born to save her brother."

"That's not fucking true. That wasn't the only reason she was born. Her parents love her."

I love her.

"Kai," he says, his voice very serious. "I'm just telling you that Theo looks like he's out for blood. His father is tough on him, and his father always gets his way, and what he wants is for his son to be with a good girl like Jami. I'm just giving you the heads up, okay?"

I nod, and exhale a harsh breath. "Okay, I appreciate it."

"Fighting with him won't be good for you, but I think he's going to do whatever it takes to knock you down and win her back."

"I know." I'd fight him though. If it means protecting Jami from him, I'd be happy to introduce my fist to his face.

He steps close and puts his hand on my shoulder. "You don't want to blow your chances in the NHL, my friend."

I nod as I try to control the anger rising up in me. It's been brewing all day, since my run in with Theo's mom, and it's a bit scary how fast I think I could snap.

"We'd better get back out there," I say, and I go out the door first. We walk down the hall in silence and I have to say, I appreciate my roommate—my friend—having my back. Even though we come from rival high schools, we're both on the same team now, on and off the ice.

I keep my head down and go straight back to the table, and everyone is laughing at something Brad said. Jami arches a brow when she sees me, checking to see if I'm good, and while I'm not, I give her a nod and smile.

I bite into my dessert, and try to follow along with the conversation. "The pie is good," I mention.

Kellan glances at me. "You call this pie?"

"What? It's good," I say and laugh.

"It's from the local grocery store. Come to my restaurant next weekend, Kai. I'll make you a real pumpkin pie."

I nod. Next weekend, my month with Jami is up. I steal a fast glance at her to gauge her reaction to the invitation, but she's not looking at me. She's looking over my head at someone or something behind me, and my stomach cramps for two reasons. Maybe she really is done when our month is up, and maybe what she's currently looking at is her ex.

I resist the urge to turn. If I see Theo watching her, I might get up and punch him in the face. "Yeah, I'll come by next weekend," I tell Kellan.

I wipe my mouth with my napkin and set it on the table, ready to get the fuck out of this place. I want Jami alone, in her bed. Tonight. Tomorrow. Forever.

Derek rubs his stomach. "I think I ate too much. How about we go for a walk and work the calories off?" he asks Claire.

She sets her napkin on the table. "I think that's a great idea." She smiles at her children. "Anyone want to join us?"

Kellan mumbles something under his breath about other ways to work off the calories and I bite my bottom lip when Claire leans in and inquires, "Sorry, what was that?"

"Nothing, Mom."

I catch Jami's grin, and arch a brow to let her know I have the same idea as her brother. Kellan and Brad stand, and Jami and I follow them up.

"We'll see you later tonight, then," Claire says.

"Probably not," Kellan mumbles again, taking Brad's hand.

I walk the long length of the table, my eyes on Jami as I go. When we reach the end, I take her hand in a possessive move. Yes, it's to show everyone—especially Theo—that she's with me.

"I have to dart to the men's room first," Kellan says.

Brad nods. "Me too."

"Let's get out of here," I say to Jami and she readily agrees. We step from the mess hall and go down the stairs. Lots of folks are standing around chatting, and we grab our coats from the rack and head outside.

"I never thought that would be over," she whispers and lets loose a relieved breath.

"You didn't have fun?"

"I only go because Mom and Dad want me there."

I nod, and it reminds me what Thomas said about her being a good girl, and obedient, just the kind of girl Theo's dad wants for his son. Assholes. I want Jami to climb trees, throw axes, and experience life. I want everything for her.

We start toward the sidewalk when the doors bang open behind us. Jami jumps, her hand going to her chest. I turn and every nerve in my body jumps to life, when I see Theo and a bunch of his asshole friends coming our way. Fuck man, this isn't good.

"Jami, go home," I say and put her behind me.

"Kai, no. I'll go back inside and get help."

If she goes back inside, she has to walk by Theo and I don't trust him not to grab her. "It's going to be okay, just go home. I'll meet you there." As I try to get her to leave, I square off against douche bag. "What the fuck do you want?"

"I want my girl back."

"She's not your girl."

He snorts. "Oh, you think she's yours. She only agreed to this to make me jealous." He tries to look around me. "It's okay, baby. It worked. I want you, and only you." Jami makes a whimpering noise behind me and I'm two seconds from knocking Theo out for scaring her, when Kellan and Brad come out the door behind them.

"What's going on?" Kellan asks.

Theo glances at the two over his shoulder. "Nothing, faggot, mind your own business."

Brad circles Theo and stands beside me. He's a big bastard, and not a guy anyone wants to mess with. He cracks his knuckles. "What did you say?"

Theo doesn't look so sure of himself anymore. "This doesn't have anything to do with you."

"If you're messing with my teammate and calling my boyfriend names, I'd say it has everything to do with me." He widens his legs, ready for battle.

"Look, Jami," Theo cajoles, his voice not as confident as it was minutes ago. "This bet is up in one week. Don't think this was anything more than a bet. You don't mean anything to this asshole. When you don't serve a purpose anymore, he'll dump you. You'll see."

"You're fucking wrong," I blurt out. "I love her." Small hands grip the back of my coat and tug. Goddammit, I didn't want her to hear me tell her I love her like this.

"You love her? Give me a fucking break, Kai. You're just saying that to piss me off."

It takes every ounce of strength I have not to call him on his shit. But I don't want to voice what I learned from Thomas. I don't want to hurt Jami. I won't.

"You know I can take better care of her than you, Kai." He takes a small step forward, despite the way Brad is widening his stance, prepared for battle. "In your heart you know that, right?" Theo juts his chin out and smirks at me. "You also know in your heart how good you are at taking care of those you love. You know I'm right. Don't you, BM?"

And that's when the first punch of the night is thrown —by me.

23

JAMI

From the wooden chair in Kai's parents' kitchen, I finish the last mouthful of coffee in my mug and stand to put it in the dishwasher.

"Oh, I've got that. You guys need to get on the road," Marie says as she puts my mug in the dishwasher. A frown mars her pretty face as she looks out the kitchen window as the rain pelts the glass. She frowns. "The weather doesn't look great. I don't think it's letting up, Kai," she tells him as he comes into the kitchen with our bags. He frowns, much like his mother, and my throat tightens. I realize he doesn't like driving in inclement weather since the accident, and I'm pretty sure he's been stalling our departure, waiting for the heaviest rains to let up. Of course, he hasn't said that. He hasn't said much of anything all day.

The truth is he's been antsy, jittery, and I'm not sure if it's because of what happened yesterday with Theo's mother at the orchard, or if it's because he got into it with Theo outside the mess hall. Both of those incidents brought back his painful past, and it's easy to tell it's shaken him to his core again. Being back here in the valley where the accident happened doesn't help either.

But, I can't forget, he did tell Theo he loved me—which shocked and thrilled me—even though he's not brought it up since. Our plan to head back to my place for a little quiet bedroom time was a bust because Theo also got in a few good punches that left Kai with a split lip and a swollen eye. At least I think that's why Kai told me he had a headache and went to sleep. I used that time for studying, but I would rather have been snuggling with him.

Then again, maybe he pushed me away because he thinks Theo was right, and he can't take care of those he loves. Of course, there's the small insecure part of me that does worry he only said he loved me to piss Theo off. God, I just don't know what to think anymore, and now as we pack up our things from his parents place, to get ready to go home, he doesn't look like he's much in the mood for talking. It's going to be a hell of a long, uncomfortable drive.

"Do you want to take a bag of ice with you?" Marie asks, her worried gaze moving over his swollen eye.

"No, I'm good," he grumbles and Marie gives me an uneasy glance.

"I can drive," I tell him. "If you need to rest your eye."

"You can't drive a stick," he reminds me through clenched teeth.

"Oh, right."

"I don't want to be responsible for you missing your test tomorrow."

I nod, but I think he's trying to prove Theo wrong—that he can and will take care of me.

"We'll take the old road." He always takes the old road between Greenwood and Middleton and I know it's not because he has a black eye. It's because it's that stretch of provincial highway where he went off the road with Coop and he can avoid it, using the old road.

Bill comes into the kitchen. "It sure is coming down hard out there. Do you want me to drive you guys to the city?"

The muscles in Kai's jaw clench so hard, I'm worried he's going to break his teeth. His eyes harden. "You don't think I can get her back safely?" he asks, his tone harsh and accusing. But underneath those surface emotions, I sense his fears, his insecurities. His father's head rears back, his mother's jaw drops, and my eyes grow wide. Theo and his mother really got into his head.

"Kai, son. My truck is big and heavy. I just thought it would be easier to negotiate the roads in the rain. Our stretch of highway has terrible ruts."

Kai's shoulders relax and he shakes his head. "Yeah, sorry, Dad. Just ah...headache."

Marie goes to the cupboard and pulls out a bottle of meds. "Here take these with you."

Kai nods and puts them in his bag, and I notice he doesn't have a coat on as he hands me mine.

"Where's your coat?" I ask.

"In the bag."

I don't say more. Instead, I turn to Marie. "Thank you so much for dinner. It was delicious."

"Are you sure you guys don't want leftovers?"

"I think I've had enough turkey for a while," I say and she laughs.

"Let me help you with those bags," Bill says and Kai moves away.

"No, it's okay. You don't need to get wet. I got it."

We walk to the door, and I thank them again before Kai pulls it open and the rain falls in buckets. "On the count of three?" I ask and he nods. He hits the fob to unlock his jeep and I run to the passenger side while he takes his time, getting completely soaked as he puts the bags in the back and slides into the driver's seat.

"You'll have to teach me to drive a stick," I say as he starts up his vehicle.

He slicks his wet hair from his forehead. "I can if you want."

I turn on the heater. He must be freezing from the cold rain, and his clothes are wet. He turns the vehicle in the big driveway and we start out on the old road. He's going slow enough, his wipers on high, but it's damn hard to see through the downpour.

Water is racing along the ditches, and spilling onto the road from Jacob's Creek, which tends to flood a lot in heavy rain. "This is crazy. Maybe we should wait until tomorrow."

He's gripping the steering wheel so tight, I'm sure his hands must hurt. "Once we get off the side roads, we should be okay," he assures me, and I know as soon as we're past the two lane stretch of highway with the ruts, the section where his best friend was killed, I think we'll be fine too.

I push back in my seat, and try to relax as he stays laser focused on the road ahead. We drive for about fifteen minutes, and his entire body goes stiff when up ahead we see flashing lights. I put my hand on his knee, my heart thumping, "What's going on?"

He doesn't look at me, doesn't take his eyes off the road as he answers with, "I don't know."

"I hope it's not an...accident." As soon as that word leaves my mouth a strange, strangled noise catches in his throat. There's nothing good about this is good. Nothing good at all. "Maybe we should go back. Head to the city early tomorrow morning."

He nods, like he agrees, and slows as we approach a police car. An officer comes up to us, and signals for us to roll down the window. Kai obliges and the officer shines his flashlight into the car.

"Bad night to be out here," he says, checking us both out.

"We're just headed to the city," Kai explains. "We were home for Thanksgiving."

The police officer leans in. "I'm afraid you're going to have to get on the highway, the bridge is closed up ahead."

Kai swallows. "We'll just turn around and go back the same way." The officer puts his hand on a square mic on his shoulder and exchanges words I can't hear. He finishes and shakes his head. "Nope can't do that either. Just got word there's too much flooding near Jacob's creek." He shines his light toward the exit that leads to the highway. "Jump on the highway and you can backtrack from there."

"Kai," I whisper quietly. "We can just pull over and wait it out."

"You need to get moving," the officer states.

Kai nods and rolls up his window. He takes a couple of breaths, glances over his shoulder and swerves around the officer. He gets on the highway, and starts the drive back to his place. I keep my hand on his leg, letting him know everything is going to be okay.

"We could just pull off the road here."

"No, it's too dangerous. Up ahead, there's an old logging road, we'll pull off there and wait this out. I'm sorry, Jami. We shouldn't even have left the house."

"You were just trying to get me back for my test."

"I should have known better." He pounds on the wheel and my heart jumps into my throat because I know exactly what's going through his head. "Why didn't I know better?" he mumbles.

Kai glances into his rearview mirror as a truck, I think it's a big farming truck, comes speeding up from behind.

"What is wrong with people?" I ask.

A truck comes toward us in their lane, but as he flies by it splashes water on the windshield. The wipers are on high as it is, but not even that is enough to clear it. Kai blinks numerous times, and it's easy to tell he's having a hard time seeing, especially considering one eye is swollen.

Before he can get his window cleared enough to see the road ahead, the big truck behind us passes us in a no-pass zone, heading into oncoming traffic, but he's speeding so I guess he thinks he can make it.

Water splashes up again, and Kai hits the brakes to slow us before the farm truck collides with the vehicle headed toward him, but our tires must hit a rut, because the next thing I know, we're hydroplaning and out of control.

I hear screaming, only to realize I'm the one doing it as I brace my hands on the dashboard. Kai curses and tries to get control of the vehicle, but when the tires hit pavement again, he loses all control and we go off the road.

All I remember hearing is crunching sounds and the car tumbling, coming to stop in the ditch, and I'm happy to see it's upright. I take a couple of deep breaths, mentally checking to see if I'm okay, and then I begin to move body parts, shifting to see Kai.

His head is against the steering wheel, and my heart nearly jumps out of my chest. "Kai," I manage to get out as my throat tightens. "Kai," I yell again, my voice nearly bordering on hysteria when he doesn't move.

Do I touch him, move him, shake him? As a million questions go through my rattled brain, I tentatively reach out to Kai, only to pull my hand back, because that's when I realize I need to call for help. I reach down to my feet, fumbling around on the floor until I find my bag. The car is dark, making it impossible to see anything, my brain so panicked my fingers aren't working properly.

When I can't readily find my phone, a pained noise crawls out of my throat, and it's followed by a moan from the driver's seat.

"Kai," I cry out. "Are you okay?" My fingers connect with my phone, and I'm seconds from calling 911 when sirens sound in the distance. "Kai."

"Jami," he answers, his voice low and strained as he pushes himself off the steering wheel. I can't see him well enough to know if he's bleeding and that's when I realize something is dripping down my face, but I'm pretty sure it's tears and not blood. "What..."

"We went off the road," I tell him, assuming he has a concussion and isn't really remembering anything right now. "Sirens...police are coming. Are you hurt? Can you move? Is anything broken?"

"Are you hurt?" he asks, panic clear in his voice.

"No, I'm okay. But I'm worried about you. Do you think anything is broken?"

He hisses as I shoot more questions at him, and as I try to look him over, his future in the NHL, or lack thereof—flashes before my eyes. Ohmigod, what if he destroyed his body and can't fulfill his dream—Coop's dream?

God, he's going to blame himself for this. Just like he blamed himself for Coop's death. But none of this is his fault. Some idiot practically ran us off the road. But knowing Kai, he'll blame himself because he had something to prove, to Theo, me, and to himself, that he could take care of me, and now, this accident is going to set him back years.

"Kai, it was an accident," I mumble, as the sirens grow louder. He says something in response, but it's garbled, and I can't quite make it out. Voices sound in the distance, and I reach for Kai, put my hand on his arm. "We need to get you to the hospital."

A beat of silence and then, he orders, "Go home, Jami."

Those three cold words, and the curt way they were delivered, curl down my spine and sends shards of ice through my blood. "Kai?" I ask my voice breathless as my heart hammers.

"What are you saying? I'm not going home. I'm going to the hospital with you."

"Call your parents and tell them to come and get you."

This time his words hit like a slap to the face, and my head rears back.

"Kai, no. I know what you're doing—"

"Good, then you know our month is almost over, so let's just end this charade now."

Kai's door is pulled open and light shines into the car. "Are you two okay?"

"I am, but Kai needs to go to the hospital," I blurt out quickly. Honestly, I'm not okay. Not emotionally or mentally anyway, but I can't think about that when Kai is hurt and clearly not in his right mind. He's in shock, saying things he doesn't mean or feel right?

Someone reaches in and unhooks Kai's seatbelt as my door is pulled open. Hands reach around me and just before Kai is moved, he whispers, "Just..."

"Just what?" I ask, clinging to his words and hoping he realizes he's closing himself off again, but this wasn't his fault, it was an accident.

"Don't go back to Theo. He's not a good guy for you."

"Kai. Please. Don't."

He's pulled from the car, but not before he adds, "I'm not a good guy for you either, Jami."

24

KAI

It's been almost one week since the accident and I've been laying low, skipping classes and practice, and mostly sitting in the dark, trying to recover from my concussion. Lots of people have been checking in on me, but I'm not in the mood to talk to any of them.

Honestly, I still can't wrap my brain around the fact that I was rerouted off the secondary highway only to tumble into a ditch during a fucking rainstorm, just miles from where I killed my best friend. If Jami had been hurt... I swallow down the sharp pain in my throat, unable to let my thoughts go there. Why the fuck did I get involved with her anyway? It was a big mistake. Imagine if something had happened to her —because of me. I could never have lived with myself.

Jesus Christ, how could I ever have thought that I could make it work with her? I only hurt the people I love, and while she might have come out of this accident unharmed, what about the next one, or the one after that? I'm better off closing myself off, because she's better off without me. I guess

I have to accept that I'm cursed with hurting the people I love.

As every muscle in my body squeezes tight, on high alert, I sit up in my bed. The headaches and spinning have stopped, a good sign I'm on the mend, but that doesn't mean I'm ready to get out in the real world again. While my entire world has gone to shit, I guess one good thing came out of this week. Coach called to tell me Edmonton wanted to sign me, and for a while there, when I was with Jami, I thought that it would make me happy, but the true reality is, I don't deserve happiness.

I listen for any sounds in the house, and when I'm met with silence, I push from my bed, pull on my sweats and a hoodie and pull my curtains back to look outside. It's gray and dark, and it looks like snow is coming. Good, let it snow. The cold will help numb me.

I snatch my phone off my nightstand and check it, finding numerous messages from people in my social circle. None from Jami, though, and I blink my eyes shut and try to dispel the hurt on her face when I told her to go home. God, I fucking gutted her, but doesn't she know she's better off without me. I just pray to God she doesn't go back to Theo. As much as I'd like to tell her he was using her, I can't hurt her like that.

Ah, but you've hurt her worse than that, dude.

Fuck me.

I walk across my room, open the door and once I'm sure I'm alone, I tromp downstairs and head to the kitchen. The silence is deafening as I shove a coffee pod into the machine and glance around. The place seems so empty without Jami's presence, but it's better that way. She's safer without me.

I stare out the back window, looking at nothing as I wait for my coffee to brew and once it's done, I drink it down in three big gulps, ignoring the way it burns my throat, and then set my cup in the sink. Foregoing food, since I haven't been hungry in a long time, I walk to the front door and pull it open. A cool breeze rushes inside and I let it chill my body. I tug on a pair of boots and step into the cold day, leaving my coat behind.

Walking aimlessly, I head down to the waterfront, which is busy this Saturday morning, people coming and going from the market and craft shows. Off in the distance, kids play on the playground equipment, and two dogs bark as they pass each other. I walk past the iconic blue wave sculpture that kids climb on, despite the warning sign, and make my way to the huge set of stairs that lead directly into the Halifax harbor. I drop down onto the cold cement step, where the water laps inches from my feet.

My gaze strays to the ferry that transports passengers from Halifax to Dartmouth, and let the cold air wrap around me. Only problem is, it's not quite numbing me like it used to. Christ, maybe after falling in love with Jami, I won't be able to go back to being numb. I sit there and try to call on my anger, because that always helped me in the past.

"Hey."

I turn at the sound of Bree's voice, shocked to see her standing there with two cups of coffee from Kellan's restaurant in her hands.

"Bree," I say, unable to hide the surprise in my voice.

"Mind if I join you?"

"Actually, I kind of want to be alone."

She hesitates for a second, and just when I think she's going to leave—and yes, I'm being an asshole—she sits.

"Here." She shoves the coffee into my hands, and I nod and accept it. Silence lingers between us as people hurry along the boardwalk, rushing off to their favorite restaurants or shops. I exhale as we both stare out over the water.

"You should go," I tell her, finally breaking the quiet. "It's cold."

"You're the one not dressed for it," she shoots back.

"I'm fine."

"Are you, Kai?" she challenges, and I turn to take in the seriousness on her face. "Are you really fine?"

"What are—"

She holds her hand up to stop me and I fall silent. "I'm tired of your bullshit," she says, and my head rears back. Okay, what the hell is this all about? The Bree I know is sweet and kind and gentle and completely easygoing.

"I don't know why I ever had a crush on you." She snorts out a laugh. "For years, actually."

"Bree—"

"I'm not done."

She adjusts her wool hat—wait, that's my wool hat. One I made. Where the heck did she get it? Then I remember Jami in the socks I made. That was the night she came to my bed, and opened her body to me. Jesus, she was perfect.

I tear my gaze from the hat and Bree explains, "I stopped by to see you. Thomas let me in. I was cold, and I forgot my hat, so I borrowed yours. He's just as worried about you as I am, Kai."

"No one needs—"

"Did I say that statement needed an answer from you?" Since I'm scared to speak, I just shake my head.

"As I was saying, I don't know why I ever had a crush on you." She glares at me, daring me to speak. "You never even called me your friend. I was always just the girl you knew from freshman year. Do you have any idea how much that hurt?" She glares again, and then says, "You can answer."

"Bree, I'm sorry. I didn't…I'm a fucked-up mess. I was…"

"Scared. I get it." She shakes her head and glances upward, like the sky holds all the answers to the puzzle that is me. "I get so much now. All the things you never told me. Never trusted me enough to tell me."

"I never meant to hurt you."

"But you did, Kai. You think keeping your distance is what keeps others safe, and your heart protected. But it's actually the opposite. You hurt us by pushing us away, and it hurts you too. Opening yourself up and bringing us in is what brings everyone comfort and healing. We're here for you. So many of us have been here for you. You've just closed yourself off from us."

"You shouldn't be here for me, not after the way I treated you."

"But we are, Kai. That must tell you how much you mean to us." I press my knuckles into my eyes. Christ, I could fucking sob. "I see the way you are with Jami."

My chest squeezes tight. "Please, don't."

Ignoring me, she continues. "Do you know Jami was terrified of falling for you because she thought it would hurt me and she didn't want to do that to me? You know how she handled the situation?"

"How?" I ask, risking her yelling at me again.

"She dug deep, found the courage, and talked to me. She opened up. She brought me in. She made me realize just how perfect you two were for each other. It gave me comfort, and the truth is, I love you so much, Kai, that all I ever wanted was for you to be happy. If loving Jami makes you happy, then it makes me happy."

I put my arm around her and pull her close. "I…I love you too, Bree."

"Don't let Brennan hear you say that. I'm with him now." I open my mouth to explain, and she nudges me, a grin on her face. "I know, you love me as a friend, and I love you as a friend too." My gaze moves over her face, and she adds, "We are friends, right?"

"Best friends," I tell her. "I'm happy for you and Brennan."

A line forms in her forehead as she frowns. "I'm not happy with you, though."

My stomach tightens as I take in the worry in her eyes. "Bree." A big gulping sound catches in my throat. Jesus, if I could only call on numbness and anger again.

She takes my coffee from me, sets it on the step and captures my hand in hers. "I'm tired of you hurting people, but mostly, I'm tired of you hurting yourself, Kai. You deserve happiness. You might not know it, but underneath all this anger and pain, you're a pretty great guy with a pretty great heart." I open my mouth and she shakes her head. "Don't even tell me you don't deserve it," she warns, her head cocking and her eyes narrowing, knowing I was about to do just that. A beat passes between us and then in a softer voice, she says, "I get it, you lost your best friend in an accident. That's brutal, Kai. Totally brutal. Then you thought you hurt Jami in a similar accident and it scared you. But life is scary, and it's definitely not easy, but what is the point of living it if you're only going through the motions?"

I swallow, remembering how Jami told me life was scary, as well. She also said being scared is better than being angry and alone all the time.

Jami was scared of many things, yet she took a chance on me after believing she was only brought into this world to save her brother. She took a chance on me after I—and Theo, God I'm no better than him—treated her like a commodity with our bet. She took so many chances on me, opening herself up when she, too, was afraid, and I tossed her away, making her feel like she wasn't important at all, when in fact she's the most important woman in the world to me.

Jesus, she is so much braver than I am. Wasn't I the one who said she was my responsibility for the month, when in fact it's been the opposite? She's been there for me at every turn. I lean forward and press my palms into my eyes.

"I thought I was doing better. I thought I was stronger. Jami made me stronger and in that rainstorm, I wanted to prove to her that I could be the man she needed but I was wrong."

"You are the man she needs, and the only one who doesn't believe that is you."

"But...she can't believe that now, Bree."

"Try her."

No way would Jami still believe in me. "I really fucked up."

"Yeah, Kai. You did."

"I ruined everything."

"You were scared," she tells me. "Jami knows that, but that doesn't mean she's not hurting. You pushed her away, made her feel like a pawn in all this. In her heart, I'm sure she knows that's not true, but maybe she needs to hear the truth from you."

"The truth…," I mumble under my breath. "I wasn't lying when I told Theo I loved her."

She smiles for the first time since sitting. "I had a long talk with Kellan when I went to get us coffee. He told me Jami hasn't been in the city all week. She's with her parents."

My heart constricts and my chest is so tight, it's almost impossible to take in air. "She's not going to talk to me," I croak out, my voice sounding strained and tortured, even to my own ears.

She arches a brow, a challenge in her kind eyes. "Are you telling me you're too scared to find out?"

25

JAMI

Needing to expel some excess energy even though it's drizzling—heck, it's been raining all week—I jog the perimeter of the ballfield, wanting to exhaust myself. I haven't been sleeping well, naturally, and I'm hoping the fresh air and exercise will help. I want to get in at least one good night's sleep before I head back to the city—to reality—tomorrow. I can't keep hiding at home forever. I have school, curling, and obligations. But I need my strength, otherwise, I'm going to break down and cry if I run into Kai, and chances are I'll run into him at some point.

His friends have been texting me, especially Bree. I pull my phone from my pocket, tucking it under my coat to keep it dry as I slow my run, and my heart aches as I read through her messages. The lump that's been in my throat since last weekend grows bigger as I look at her worried words. But what now? Now that Kai and I are through, how can I stay friends with his friends, if he's even going to call them that now?

My biggest worry is that Kai's going to crawl back into that dark hole he's been in for years, keeping everyone who cares about him circling it, with no way in. Tears pool in my eyes, making the wet ground blur before me. Deciding I'd better get home before I fall head first on the hard, soggy ballfield, I take a breath and force one leg in front of the other.

A figure starts toward me, tall, broad, and fast. Despite the rain and the tears blurring my view, I instantly know who it is, and I know I don't want to talk to him. He too has been messaging me, but I have nothing to say to the man who never treated me like I had any value, other than what I could do for him.

"Jami," Theo calls out, and I glance over my shoulder, wondering if I could make it to the Royal Canadian Legion building behind me and hide in the washroom until he leaves. But no, I'm tired of hiding from the world. I've been sheltered enough, I realize that's only because my parents cared, but I'm a grown woman—one who knows what she wants, even if I can't have it—and now it's time to stand on my own two feet.

"What can I do for you, Theo?" I ask. To think all I ever wanted was to be seen by this man, to be loved by him, and to be important to him. I thought I was all those things with Kai, and who am I kidding? I was. I have no doubt about that. But his old demons consumed him again, which is why he pushed me away. I don't need a degree in psychology to understand that.

"Hey, where have you been?"

"I've been here." I walk past him and he turns, jogging to catch up to me.

"You haven't been answering my texts."

I shove my wet hands into my pockets. "I know."

"Babe—"

"Don't call me that, Theo. I'm not your babe. Now if you'll excuse me, I have things to do."

He hardens a bit, not used to seeing me like this. "He was only ever using you, Jami. I told you that."

"If you're here to say you told me so, duly noted." I don't care what he has to say. He doesn't know a thing about Kai, or me, or himself.

"I want you back," he blurts out.

I snort out a laugh, and judging from the way his face is hardening, he doesn't much appreciate the way I'm dismissing him. I don't blame him. It's rude. Which makes me wonder why I allowed him to do it to me so much.

Oh, because you wanted to be loved, Jami.

"Right, that," I mumble.

"What?"

"Nothing."

"Jami, come on. We can work things out."

I stop walking and face him, letting the rain soak my cheeks. "Kai wasn't the one using me, Theo." I poke his chest. "You were."

He jolts back. "I have no idea what you're talking about."

I plant my hands on my hips. "Why me?" He angles his head, confused. "Why did your father want you dating me?"

He falters a bit. "I, uh, I have no idea what you're talking about."

"Yeah, you said that." I stare at him, not even really upset or hurt. I simply don't have feelings for Theo anymore and a part of me wonders if I ever did. "Let me guess. I was a good girl. Obedient. Submissive. The kind of girl who would follow you around and support our family when we had one."

"What's wrong with that?"

"Not a thing." I shake my head. "It's perfectly fine, if that's what a woman wants, what a couple wants. My mother stayed home and so did yours." I stare at him. "But did you ever ask me what I wanted, Theo?"

"I thought you wanted a family, and you'd do social work until that happened. Then you'd stay home, like our mothers did."

"Right." I snort out another laugh. "You never asked."

"Fine." He folds his arms and glares at me. "If that's what you need from me." He waves a hand back and forth between the two of us. "To make this right again. What do you want, Jami?"

I just shake my head, because I don't need or want a damn thing from this man and nothing he does or says can ever make it right.

"I want Kai Ward."

His face goes hard, and he grabs my arm hard. "He's no good for you. He's a fucking loser and a murderer. You're just lucky he didn't kill you the other night."

I stare at his hand on my arm. "Take your hand off me right now." I shift my stance, ready to kick him right between the legs, and he must know it's seconds from coming, because he lets go and backs up.

"You're making a mistake," he tells me, his voice harsh.

"I've made many, and right now you're making one if you think I'm ever going back to you. But don't worry, Theo. I'm sure daddy will find you the perfect wife. It's just not going to be me."

With that I turn my back on him and start walking, keeping my head high. But one thing I just said sticks in my brain. What do I want? I know the answer to that, and dammit, I am done waiting for love. Heck, I waited long enough for it from Theo. I'm not waiting anymore. I'm going to go get it. Demons be damned. If I can stand up to a six-foot, muscular hockey player, Kai's demons don't stand a chance.

With my heart racing, I walk quicker, a plan forming in my brain, but as I approach my house I glance into my backyard, only to find a big, muscular figure in the tree, my heart nearly jumps from my chest. My steps slow. What the ever-loving hell is Kai doing in my backyard tree?

"Kai?" I call out. "What are you doing?"

"Just hanging out," he yells back. "Watching you jog the ballfield."

He must have also seen me talking to Theo. "It's raining. Get down from there before you fall and crack your skull open." As soon as the words leave my mouth, my steps slow again. Kai is in my tree. Kai never liked when I climbed any tree because he avoids dangerous situations. He pushed me from his life because he thought he'd put me in a dangerous situation.

Kai is in my tree. But right now, his actions are about so much more. He's sending me a very important message, and dammit, I'm listening.

"Kai," I say again, tears welling in my eyes as my throat burns. The dog walking club, all dressed in their raingear, slow as they see me looking up at a grown-ass man in my backyard tree. I can't even imagine the rumors. I shake my head, open the gate to my backyard and step inside.

"You want to come up?" he asks, a vulnerable yet adorable look on his handsome face.

"Kai," I say again, and as I stand there, tears falling down my cheeks, he climbs down from the tree. "What...what are...?"

"I love you," he whispers, stepping up to me and putting his hands on my arms. "I'm tired of being afraid, Jami. My biggest fear was losing you, and well, that happened. What else is there to be afraid of? Well, actually a lot, but I'd rather be afraid with you, than be afraid without you."

"Kai, I...I want to be in your life. You must know that. Accidents happen, they're going to happen. But I can't stay packaged in bubble wrap." I laugh and shake my head. "Been there, done that and it's not fun."

"I want you to live the life you want, Jami. I want you to climb trees, throw axes and go on worldwide adventures. I want to do all those things with you. You deserve to live your life to the fullest, with whoever you want to live that life with." A hint of worry and fear move across his face.

I exhale. "You saw me with Theo."

He nods, and glances down. I lift his chin. "Kai, I'm not getting back with him, if that's what you're worried about."

"I actually never thought you were," he answers quietly as he looks around, staring at the ground as he puts his hands in his pockets and takes them out again, like he just doesn't know what to do with them. I touch his arm to bring his attention back to me.

"Kai?"

"I was going to go beat the shit out of him when I saw him grab your arm, but then I remembered you could take care of yourself."

I grin at that. "I can take care of myself, but I also like when you take care of me."

"Do you think I can take care of you, Jami?" There's real hope and worry in his eyes as they move over my face.

"Allowing you to take care of me isn't about being submissive or a pushover. It's about me trusting you and sharing myself with you. It's about me loving you, and you loving me."

He swallows hard. "You love me?"

"Of course, I love you, Kai."

He picks me up and hugs me tight, his lips landing on mine for a deep soul-searching kiss. When he sets me down again, I ask, "If you weren't worried about me going back with Theo, what were you worried about?" I ask pointedly, wanting an answer from him.

"Can we just forget that, and talk about you loving me?"

That's when it hits me and I gasp. "You knew."

"Knew what?" he asks and runs a shaky hand through is hair.

"You knew he was using me. You knew he wanted to be with me because I was the kind of girl his father wanted him with."

"Jami, I love you." Panic races over his face. "Don't listen to anything he has to say."

I back up on shaky legs until I reach the picnic table and drop down. "You didn't tell me."

"Jami, please." He hurries to me and drops to his knees, sliding between my thighs. "I didn't want anything he did to hurt you. I didn't want you to think you had no value. You do. You're the most important person in the world to me."

My heart swells in my chest and I smile at him. "Which is why you protected me from getting hurt."

He nods. "Yes."

I cup his face. "If you ever thought you couldn't protect me, Kai. You were wrong. You carried this hurtful secret in your heart to protect mine and that means the world to me."

"I didn't do a very good job if you found out."

"It's kind of my job to see beneath the surface, Kai. Once I pulled back the veil and allowed myself to look beneath the surface of the Theo situation, it was easy to see why he was with me. I also know why you pushed me away."

He drops his head and rests it on my legs. "I'm so fucking sorry. I'm an asshole. I was just so—"

"So, in love with me that it scared the hell out of you."

His head lifts. "Yes. Do you forgive me?"

"You don't need my forgiveness, Kai. I was never upset with you. You need your own forgiveness for Coop."

"You're right." He takes a deep breath, and when he lets it out, he says, "I forgive myself." I can almost feel the last of his survivor's guilt leave his body as I cup his cheeks and lightly brush my lips over his.

I break the kiss. "Just so you know, Kai. I was coming for you. Before I even knew you were in my tree, I was about to jump into my car and fight your damn demons."

He makes a fist and lightly nudges my chin. "That's my social worker."

"No, that's your girlfriend," I say, and he laughs.

"Right, that's my girlfriend, and I'm your boyfriend. Next year, though, when I'm in Edmonton—"

"Kai," I squeal before he can finish. "You were signed?"

"I was signed," he tells me with a smile.

"Why didn't you open with that?" I yell, so excited for him.

"I opened with 'I love you'. That's more important than anything."

My heart thumps because it shows me just how much he's grown as a person. His entire life was hockey, for Coop, but now, he's learning to love and not just me. He's loving himself, and figuring out his priorities and what makes him happy.

"Wait, what were you going to say about next year?"

"I was going to say that next year, when I'm in Edmonton, I don't think we should call each other girlfriend or boyfriend." My heart stalls for a brief second, but no, he can't be reverting back to the Kai who bet on me. "I'd like us to call each other fiancé and fiancée, or better yet, husband and wife."

"Kai," I whisper and start crying. "Are you asking—"

"Yes, I'm asking you to marry me, Jami. I love you and want to spend the rest of my life with you." He holds my face in his big, gentle hands. "But I need to know what you want. If you want a family, or if you don't. Either is fine. I want to know if you want to stay here and work or if you want to move with me. Either is fine. We can make anything work, as long as we're in it together."

The fact that he's asking fills my heart with even more love. "Yes, to everything."

A big grin spreads across his face, then he frowns. "Wait, I don't—"

"I'm so proud of you, Kai. You worked so hard to get to the NHL and no one deserves it more than you." I kiss him. "Right now, all I know is that I want to be your wife. I'm not sure if I want a family, or where I want to work. Or even if I'll work if I do have a family."

"You don't have to make any decisions right now." He crinkles his nose as rain drips from it, and says, "Well, that's not entirely true." Still down on his knees, he pulls out a velvet box and opens it. "Will you marry me, Jami?"

"Yes," I practically shriek and as he puts the ring on my finger, the rain wetting the diamond. I sneeze and we laugh. "One thing I do know is no cats."

He chuckles. "Agreed."

"We should get inside," I say.

Kai shakes his head. "I swear to God, Coop has been making it rain all week because he's pissed off and trying to send me a message." The second he stops speaking, the rain suddenly stops and we both glance up to see a gorgeous rainbow.

"Wow," I murmur.

That's when it hits us and we both look at each other, laugh and say, "Coop," in unison.

Kai kisses me with love, and then looks at the sky again, tears in his eyes as he smiles. "Thanks for looking out for me, Coop. I love you, buddy."

Kai

ne year later:

I take my beautiful wife's hand in mine and walk through the open foyer toward the gorgeously decorated dining area where our wedding guests await us. Jami decided she wanted a small Christmas wedding here at my family's vineyard, with only our closest friends and family in attendance. While I had to work around my NHL schedule, we are, fortunately, given a small break at Christmas, which is what allowed me to make this dream come true for her.

I stop outside the large double doors leading to the dining area and turn to my wife. *My wife.* Will I ever get used to that? I have never seen her look so radiant. I touch her shoulder, lightly running my fingers over her silky flesh and admire her stunning, strapless wedding dress that showcases her beautiful curves. I cup her face in my hands and kiss her with all the love inside me.

"I can't believe you're mine," I tell her as a hush falls over the dining room, the guests waiting for our entrance as our photographer moves around us, getting pictures from all angles.

"And you didn't even have to bet on me to get me here," she teases, her eyes shining with love.

I shake my head and groan, but really, I'm so goddamn happy how this all turned out. I never should have bet on her—it was a mistake to make her feel like a commodity—but she's forgiven me and I've been having a wonderful time showing her exactly what she means to me. "You're never going to let that go, are you?" I tease back.

"You *bet* I'm not," she chuckles, and it's so light and airy, so full of happiness and joy, it wraps around my full heart and squeezes tight. As I look at her, I could sob at how happy she's made me. "Kai," she murmurs her voice full of love. "I can't believe you're mine either."

"I'm pretty sure I was always yours, Jami. The second I set eyes on you at the rink, something inside me knew we were meant to be together, forever."

"I'm so glad you scored more goals than *you know who* that night."

The *you know who*—aka douche bag—she's talking about now plays for Miami, and I'm really looking forward to giving him a few hard knocks into the boards when we play against them.

As my heart thumps harder, I gesture with a nod toward the dining room. "Are you ready for this?" Honestly, if I had it my way, I'd skip the reception and take her straight to our bridal suite.

She lightly taps my nose, but there's a small hint of concern in her voice when she whispers, "The better question is, are you ready for this?"

Jesus, I love her. Love how kind, caring and sweet she is, and how she's always there for me, always offering all her love and support. Today, on our wedding day, she knows I'm thinking of Coop and how I wish he could be here with us.

I glance into the room, and my gaze moves over the small gathering. I make eye contact with every single guest, each one of them meaning so much to us. My gaze comes to a halt when I meet the eyes of Candace and Gerald Cooper. They both smile at me, and I smile back, a warmth spreading through my soul. Thanks to Jami, who helped me fight my demons, I'm in a really good place in life, and have learned to move on from the hurt and let happy memories fill my soul. I know Coop is proud of the man I turned out to be.

I take a deep breath and let it out slowly as I turn back to my beautiful wife. "I am ready," I say, and she smiles up at me.

"Come on, you two, the food is getting cold," Kellan yells and when Brad nudges him to be quiet, I just laugh. Kellan insisted, as a wedding present, that he wanted to cater our reception, and I know he's excited to showcase the special meal he's made for us. It warms my heart and I couldn't have asked for a better brother-in-law.

"We'd better get in there," Jami says, and we turn, our fingers laced together as we step through the threshold.

Everyone stands and claps as we enter, and I give Bree, one of my very best friends in the whole world—and Jami's maid of honor—a warm smile and lightly touch her shoulder as we walk by her. She smiles back, and Brennan puts his arm around her and pulls her close. I think we'll be attending their wedding soon.

I nod to Thomas, my best man, as we reach the head of the table, I pull Jami's chair out for her. She sits, and before I drop down next to her, I take in those around the table again, so grateful that they all traveled back for our wedding, especially during the busy holiday season. After college, a lot of our friends moved for work, Jami and I included. So, I know it was no easy feat for them all to be here, but like Bree once told me, I mean a lot to them all, just like they all mean a lot to me.

Speaking of moving, Jami came to Edmonton with me, and we bought a big house together—one we'll someday fill with kids. Yes, we both decided that's what we want which is why we planted a huge tree in the backyard for them to climb. But children are for later, because Jami is currently working at the air force base, doing exactly what she dreamed of doing—helping others—and in my off season, we plan to travel and I can't wait to experience the world with her. These past few months, however, I've been working my ass off, proving myself to my team, and when I'm on the road I miss her terribly, but there's nothing better than coming home to her warmth and love.

I lift my champagne glass and hold it out, my heart so full of love I'm sure it's going to burst. Everyone reaches for theirs and does the same. "To the friends and family who are here with us today, and to the ones who are here in our hearts, thank you all for experiencing this amazing day with us."

I sit, and Thomas stands to say a few words. Once he's done, he steps up to us to clink our glasses and gives Jami a kiss on the cheek.

I look at my wife. "I love you, babe," I whisper and that's when I notice her eyes glossing over. Jesus. Thomas and his damn cat.

"The food!" Kellan yells.

Jami laughs and holds back a sneeze. "Come on, the quicker we eat the quicker we can get out of here..." She gives me a playful wink, and quietly adds, "...I feel an allergy attack coming on."

I grin, ready to give her all the immunotherapy she wants. Tonight, tomorrow, forever.

* * *

Thank you so much for reading Kai and Jami's story. I hope you loved it as much as I do. Be sure to check out the other books in the series. Up next is Deal Breaker, Hard Burn, and Fake Out.

ALSO BY CATHRYN FOX

Scotia Storms

Away Game (Rebels)

Warm Up (Rebels)

Crash Course (Rebels)

Home Advantage (Rebels)

Shut Out (Rebels)

Moving Target (Rivals)

Face Off (Rivals)

Scoring Fast (Rivals)

Opposing Teams (Rivals)

Deal Breaker (Rebels)

Hard Burn (Rivals)

Fake Out (Rivals)

End Zone

Fair Play

Enemy Down

Keeping Score

Trading Up

All In

Blue Bay Crew

Demolished

Leveled

Hammered

Single Dad
Single Dad Next Door
Single Dad on Tap
Single Dad Burning Up

Players on Ice
The Playmaker
The Stick Handler
The Body Checker
The Hard Hitter
The Risk Taker
The Wing Man
The Puck Charmer
The Troublemaker
The Rule Breaker
The Rookie
The Sweet Talker
The Heart Breaker

In the Line of Duty
His Obsession Next Door
His Strings to Pull
His Trouble in Talulah
His Taste of Temptation
His Moment to Steal
His Best Friend's Girl
His Reason to Stay

Confessions

Confessions of a Bad Boy Professor

Confessions of a Bad Boy Officer

Confessions of a Bad Boy Fighter

Confessions of a Bad Boy Doctor

Confessions of a Bad Boy Gamer

Confessions of a Bad Boy Millionaire

Confessions of a Bad Boy Santa

Confessions of a Bad Boy CEO

Hands On

Hands On

Body Contact

Full Exposure

Dossier

Private Reserve

House Rules

Under Pressure

Big Catch

Brazilian Fantasy

Improper Proposal

Boys of Beachville

Good at Being Bad

Igniting the Bad Boy

Bad Girl Therapy

Stone Cliff Series:

Crashing Down

Wasted Summer

Love Lessons

Wrapped Up

Eternal Pleasure Series

Instinctive

Impulsive

Indulgent

Sun Stroked Series

Seaside Seduction

Deep Desire

Private Pleasure

Captured and Claimed Series:

Yours to Take

Yours to Teach

Yours to Keep

Firefighter Heat Series

Fever

Siren

Flash Fire

Playing For Keeps Series

Slow Ride

Wild Ride

Sweet Ride

Breaking the Rules:

Hold Me Down Hard

Pin Me Up Proper

Tie Me Down Tight

Stand Alone Title:

Hands on with the CEO

Torn Between Two Brothers

Holiday Spirit

Unleashed

Knocking on Demon's Door

Web of Desire

ABOUT CATHRYN

New York Times and *USA today* Bestselling author, Cathryn is a wife, mom, sister, daughter, and friend. She loves dogs, sunny weather, anything chocolate (she never says no to a brownie) pizza and red wine. She has two teenagers who keep her busy with their never ending activities, and a husband who is convinced he can turn her into a mixed martial arts fan. Cathryn can never find balance in her life, is always trying to find time to go to the gym, can never keep up with emails, Facebook or Twitter and tries to write page-turning books that her readers will love.

Connect with Cathryn:
Newsletter https://app.mailerlite.com/webforms/landing/c1f8n1
Twitter: https://twitter.com/writercatfox
Facebook: https://www.facebook.com/AuthorCathrynFox?ref=hl
Blog: http://cathrynfox.com/blog/
Goodreads: https://www.goodreads.com/author/show/91799.Cathryn_Fox

Pinterest http://www.pinterest.com/catkalen/

www.ingramcontent.com/pod-product-compliance
Lightning Source LLC
Chambersburg PA
CBHW032023310726
48972CB00002B/524